Deep Breathing

A Novel

RACHAEL L. LEHMBERG

ISBN: 0692554181
ISBN 13: 9780692554180
Seal Beach, CA

DEDICATION

To my husband, David Lehmberg, the best buddy a diver ever had.

TABLE OF CONTENTS

PREFACE

"Heck of a night to go out on the ocean." Rip MacKinsey, manager and partner in MidPacific Diving Adventures, looked gloomily out of the window of his dive shop at the water front. Coconut trees bent and bobbled in the wind. "I guess we'd better cancel."

"No way. The boat payment is due tomorrow and with the eight folks we've got signed up for the night dive, we'll just make it." His partner, Jackie Cole, who had been jabbing numbers into her computer, glared at him from behind its screen. A muscle in her jaw twitched.

"So? Let the bank wait a couple of days. Safety is more important than our credit rating." Rip took another sip from his coffee cup as he gazed at the horizon where a glorious Hawaiian sunset should have been. Tonight there were only towering clouds reflected in the leaden water of Lahaina Harbor. Even from here he could hear halyards clanking against masts in the gusty wind.

"Damn it, Rip! I can't believe you sometimes!" Jackie slid off her high stool and stood up, leaning the palms of her hands on the glass topped counter. "That safety first, Boy Scout attitude of yours is going to ruin us! It's been raining since Christmas. If we wait for perfect weather we'll be bankrupt by summer."

Rip turned away from the window and faced her over the tops of the wetsuit and tee shirt racks. "Look Jackie, I know we agreed that you'd be in charge of the night dives, but we don't want anyone to get hurt. Don't be so——"

"So what? Realistic?" she snapped. Her gray eyes had hardened to the color of steel. "If you hadn't gotten so high and mighty and made me stop when you found out I was riding sea turtles on the night dives, we'd have enough money stashed in the bank so we could *afford* to be picky about the weather."

Rip sighed as he lowered himself onto the window ledge. He raked his hand through his dark wavy hair. Although he was only thirty-four, he was already going gray at the temples. Getting too old to start over. As much as he hated to admit it, she could be right. But she certainly was not right about the turtles. "Jackie," he said softly, "What's happened to you? When we decided to buy this business together, I thought you shared my ideas. We were going to take folks to see the world under the ocean, not to get rich but to show them how amazing it is. We were going to teach them to respect——"

"Teach?" Jackie snorted. "We can't teach anyone anything if we lose this business. Do you want to go back to scraping boat bottoms for a living?"

"Things aren't that bad. We'll be okay."

Rip stretched his long legs out and set his coffee cup down beside him. He took a deep breath before continuing. "Now look, I know you feel you have to show your father that you can be as successful as he is, but if we violate what we believe in, what does that make us? Besides, it's not only illegal to even touch a sea turtle it's just plain wrong. When you go in that cave at night and roust those sleeping turtles, you're putting their lives at risk."

She shook her head causing her long, blond braid to twitch like the tail of an angry cat. "C'mon Rip! Animal encounters are what people want these days—'swim with dolphins," kiss the whales—' So we ride a few turtles, it's not like we're making them into soup!"

"You might as well if you're going to kill them anyhow!" Rip could feel the blood rushing to his face so he took a moment to calm himself. When he spoke again, his voice was low, but firm. Look you know as well as I do that when you scare them awake like that, you could cause them to drown. At the very least you're chasing them away from the nesting beach."

"Oh, yeah, yeah, but--"

"No buts! He stood up immediately, his height intimidating. "Then, while I was on the Mainland last month, you not only grabbed and rode the turtles yourself, you encouraged other divers to do the same."

"Yes, I did!" Jackie's voice was suddenly shrill. "And I thought you'd be grateful that for once we finished the month with a profit!"

Recognizing the disappointment behind her fury, Rip crossed the floor in three long steps and touched her shoulder lightly.

"Look," he said, his voice softened, "We're not getting anywhere arguing. Let's compromise. We won't cancel the dive tonight, but no turtle riding! You can take the folks down and *show* them the turtles. Just look; don't touch. Okay?"

For an answer, she pressed her lips together in a hard, tight line. Rip tried not to notice. He dropped his hand and switched to a crisp, business-like voice. "So who have we got tonight? Are all these guys experienced divers?"

Jackie opened a blue folder marked "January 17" and flipped through the forms filled out in a variety of masculine scrawls. She stopped when she came to one that had been completed in a neat, rounded script.

"Looks that way, except this one. A funny name—Zephyr. She came in just before we closed."

"She?"

"Yeah, but don't worry about her. She probably weighs 90 pounds dripping wet. And 'wet' is what she's never going to be. I'll bet you two beers that she'll wimp out the minute she sees the waves at the dive site. Count on it."

"Did she fill out all the forms and give you her certification card?"

"Do you think she'd be part of the group if she hadn't?"

"No, of course not. Sorry." Rip plucked his Dodgers cap off the window ledge and jammed it on his head, pulling the visor down against the rain as he opened the front door. "I'm going to the dock to check out the boat. I'll see you at the dock. You can bring the customers down when you get them briefed."

A gust of wind blew the door shut and he found himself alone on the glistening wet sidewalk. Ducking his head, he strode in the direction of the waterfront, his thoughts troubled. Partners had to trust each other. When trust is gone, what's left?

But there wasn't time to think about it now. He had work to do.

■ ■ ■

An hour later, the forty-five foot dive boat, *Ipo Nui*, was readied and leaping at her dock lines. Ten compressed air tanks nestled in their cradles under the railings of the back deck. Everything seemed in order. Even so, Rip's mood darkened with apprehension when a blast of rain spritzed his face as he climbed the unprotected ladder to the bridge.

He shook big droplets of water off his cap, tossed it on the chart table behind him, then turned the ignition key and fired up the engines. They thundered to life instantly, quickly easing into a steady rumble. Their sound never failed to excite him. He still could hardly believe his luck that the powerful vessel really belonged to him – well, half of it, anyway. Her name, *Ipo Nui*, had been his choice. It meant "Big Sweetheart."

Flipping on the windshield wipers, he peered down at the dock through the thickening gloom. With a quick glance at his watch, he looked for Jackie. Then, in a moment she appeared followed by seven large figures and one small one – all carrying duffle bags lumpy with diving equipment. As he watched, he saw the small figure struggling with her shoulder straps, hurrying resolutely to keep up with the group.

He smiled. *Snow White and the Seven Giants. As soon as I get a chance, I'd better talk to her and make sure she's really up for this.*

Beyond the docks, the lights of Lahaina Town flickered through a curtain of rain.

1

Zepher Myers grabbed at the strap of her camera case as it slithered off her narrow shoulder. For a moment it dangled precariously over the slash of dark water between the dock and the boat. She shifted her duffle bag to her other hand and secured the camera strap back onto her shoulder. The gangplank under her feet jumped and heaved like a diabolical carnival ride.

"Whew," she said under her breath. Not only would losing her new underwater camera be distressing, but without photographic evidence Ocean Observers would have nothing except rumors of endangered species harassment to take to court. That wouldn't be enough to close down Mid-Pacific Diving Adventures. Besides, she needed photos for the article she was planning for the organization's magazine.

She'd have to be extra careful. Fatigue always made her clumsy and now the long flight from Phoenix, plus the strain of being deceptive, was making her shaky as well. Being the only woman in the group certainly didn't help her attempt to be inconspicuous! She caught up with the other divers as they followed Jackie across the deck and crowded into the cabin of the boat. Inside, the air was heavy with the odor of diesel exhaust and, as the men began to take off jackets and shirts, of sweat.

Big macho guys, she thought. *What am I doing here?*

She tried not to look at them, but in the cramped quarters a huge bicep twitched its tattooed cobra in her face. A young guy with bleached hair and a dark moustache stepped on her foot.

"Sorry, babe," he muttered.

"It's okay," she responded, keeping herself from adding, *but please don't call me "babe!"*

Amid loud voices, the men were stripping down to their swimsuits grunting as they tugged the tight neoprene wetsuits over heavily muscled legs. The rubbery sleeves flopped around like squid tentacles.

Zephyr pulled her sweatshirt over her head exposing her yellow bikini top. She could feel eyes on her but she refused to meet them. After kicking her way out of her jeans she dragged her pink and black wetsuit free of her duffle and struggled into it. Slipping an elastic band off her wrist, she restrained her long, copper-colored curls then, scooping up her mask and fins, she elbowed her way through the crowd of half-naked men and stepped out into the cold, damp wind on the back deck.

Although her stomach was tight with fear, the deep gurgling *thrum* of the marine engines, which she could both hear and feel, still set off the remembered leap of excitement in her chest. As the *Ipo Nui* lunged out of the harbor and encountered the swells of the open sea, she grabbed a railing then seated herself on one of the benches that lined the back deck. Sliding her mask and fins under it, she looked out over the roiling water. Although the ocean was an old friend to her, it was certainly a friend in a bad mood tonight. She knew it well enough to be aware that its bad moods were not to be taken lightly.

As the other divers emerged, laughing and joking and filling up the benches, she wondered if their loud voices were covering up their own anxiety about the conditions that awaited them.

There was a sudden silence. All eyes rested on the captain as he descended the ladder from the bridge. Zephyr knew immediately from the background material Ocean Observers had sent her, that he was Rip MacKinsey, one of the owners of the dive business. In person he was much better looking than she had expected from the blurry image which someone had photographed at distance. He had a swimmer's body - wide at the shoulders, narrow through the hips. His hair, tossed by the wind, was dark and softly wavy.

He glanced around at the group of divers, then his gazed rested on her. Even though his eyes were kind, she looked quickly away hoping that he would not single her out for attention.

But he did. He strode towards her. "Feeling okay?"

Zephyr flinched guiltily at the sound of his voice. He stood directly in front of her, feet wide apart to steady himself on the bounding deck.

"Sure. Great!" She avoided looking at him, but in her peripheral vision, even in the dim running lights, she was too aware of his thickly muscled thighs. His tight fitting wetsuit left little to the imagination.

"Because if you're not, we've got these acupressure bands to wear on your wrist. I know it sounds hocus-pocus, but they really work."

His voice was gentle and his eyes, when she looked up into them, showed real concern. If he knew what a fraud I am he'd probably pitch me in the ocean right now, she thought.

"No, really I'm fine."

"Okay, but are you actually planning to dive in just that light weight wetsuit?"

"Well, certainly. This is Hawaii, isn't it?" Her voice was sharper than she intended. More defensive. Something about his straight forward gaze made her nervous. Could it be her own role as an environmental spy?

She tried to focus on the sea turtles. If the anonymous tip was true and Mid Pacific had been harassing them to provide cheap thrills for adventure-craving mainlanders . . . well, Ocean Observers needed to know about it. The U.S. Fish and Wildlife officials needed to know about it. And Mid-Pacific should have its license yanked. Her assignment was the important focus now, not the thighs of the man who stood in front of her.

"Sure, it's Hawaii, but it's also January and in case your travel agent didn't tell you, it's been raining for three weeks. That water out there is colder than a . . . well, cold anyway. If you'd said something back at the dock, Jackie could've rented you something warmer."

"I'll be just fine. I've worn this suit on all my dives." She didn't add that all of them had been in Arizona and she'd been in a swimming pool. The deep end.

"Up to you. But hypothermia is nothing to fool around with." He shrugged and started to turn away, but apparently thought better of it. Bracing his forearm against the railing, he leaned over her. His eyes locked on hers and she felt her face growing hot despite the cold wind. A strand of his hair blew across his forehead and he brushed it back without interrupting his steady gaze.

"And exactly how many dives have you done since you've been on Maui?"

"My plane just landed a few hours ago," she said, trying not to sound as defensive as she felt. "I haven't had time to do anything but catch a shuttle and check into my hotel."

"And this is your first time here?"

"There has to be a first time for everything, doesn't there?"

She felt a flush race up her face. The double entendre seemed to hang in the air, charging it with a sudden sexual tension that she knew only too well was entirely inappropriate under the circumstances. Her eyes darted away from his. She was relieved when he didn't pick up on the opening she'd handed him.

"Might be a good idea to get some rest before we get to the dive site. You're welcome to use one of the bunks in the cabin."

Damn. Did he have to be so nice?

"Thank you. I think I will."

He held out his hand and helped her to her feet, steadying her with a firm touch on her shoulder while he guided her towards the cabin door. She was aware of the other divers watching her. Probably snickering. Or worse yet, feeling sorry for her - thinking she was sick. Suddenly she felt terribly vulnerable and glad for the chance to be alone for a while. Alone and out of the wind.

When she had a hold of an interior railing, he let go of her with a friendly pat on the back. Funny how comforting the small gesture was. Even through her wetsuit the spot where he'd touched her seemed to tingle.

Inside, the bunks were crowded with diving gear and duffel bags. She stumbled through the clutter and collapsed next to somebody's tee shirt. She was too tired to care about the musky smell of sweat.

Her eyelids felt gritty from the dryness of the airplane. Counting the layover in L.A. it had been ten hours and three time zones since she'd left Sky Harbor Airport in Phoenix. Kevin's passionate kiss as they parted at the gate had brought disapproving stares from some of the grandmotherly types. Strange how she herself had felt nothing. She was relieved when her row was called and she was free to walk down the jet way alone. Probably just prewedding jitters. That and the lingering irritation from the argument they'd had the night before -- after he'd given her a brushup scuba lesson.

They'd been perched on the rough cement at one end of her swimming pool. Kevin was shaking the water out of his swim mask more vigorously than necessary. "So what's the problem with divers riding on sea turtles? And

why is this such a big deal that you have to go dashing half
way around the world when we haven't even set the date
for our wedding yet?"

"Kevin, we've been over this." She'd leaned forward
and gazed at their reflections in the water. "I thought you
understood."

His pale blue eyes looked sullen. "Obviously, I don't."

"Those are endangered animals and the stress can kill
them."

"So?" Kevin stood up abruptly. "I'm sorry, I just
don't get why you've got this thing about turtles." He began unsnapping the hoses from their compressed air tanks.
He wasn't looking at her but she could see his anger in the
set of his shoulders.

Zephyr gazed into the bright rectangle of shimmering
turquoise lit from below. How could she explain that she
knew how it felt to live in a shell? To seem self-contained
but to be helplessly vulnerable? And could she ever hope
he would understand what it was like to grow up with sea
creatures as her only friends?

Kevin turned to face her. With a sharp flip of his head
he tossed his dripping blond hair to one side of his forehead. "And what I also don't get is why you're going to so
much trouble to save a few slimy reptiles."

"Haven't you been listening to me? Remember what
I told you about the sea turtles on the beach in Mexico?
How fishermen caught them and turned them upside
down for *days* until they died? I was only ten years old so
all I could do was watch. I was as helpless as they were.
And they cry tears, Kevin, real tears!"

"If I cry real tears at the airport will you stay and save me?" His tone was sarcastic but she could feel the hurt underneath. When he left, lugging the empty air tanks, the house seemed lonelier than it had since her mother's funeral. Still, if he didn't understand her feelings now, would he ever?

The question was troubling, but Zephyr could not allow herself to think about it out here in the middle of the ocean. This was her first big assignment. The staff was counting on her, the turtles needed her. And suddenly the ring on her finger felt uncomfortably tight.

■ ■ ■

She must have dozed because when Rip leaned into the cabin and called, "We're almost there. All hands on deck," she thought for a moment that she was back on her parents' sailboat in the South Pacific.

Reluctantly, Zephyr sat up. Her stomach did feel queasy now, but she ignored it and climbed out onto the deck. The wind was colder than she'd remembered. She fought the urge to draw back into the shelter of the cabin.

"Okay," Rip was saying in a deep firm voice that could be heard easily even over the roar of the diesel engines. "Everybody link up with your dive buddies. If you didn't bring a buddy, find one now. Remember, first rule of diving is --"

"Never dive alone." The response was delivered in unison by a chorus of male voices. They sounded like bored school children repeating a rule that they had been hearing since kindergarten.

"Good! That's right. Now get geared up. We'll be at the dive site in about ten minutes."

Find a partner. Zephyr glanced around. Instantly she felt like she was back in high school gym class in Phoenix - the weird new kid who'd been living on a *boat*, for God sakes!

All the guys seemed to be helping each other with their dive gear. Who wants a hundred pound weakling for a dive buddy?

They all think I'll slow them down and they're probably right.

She slid back into the place where she'd been sitting earlier and felt around under the bench for her swim fins. She didn't need anyone. Never mind what that turtle abuser says; she could do it alone.

An elbow nudged her arm.

"Hey, Honey," said a booming voice next to her, "You come with me. I'll take good care of you."

She turned and looked at the speaker, a man whose florid face she had noticed back at the dive shop while Jackie explained the use of the underwater flashlights. Thick neck, big belly. A heart attack waiting to happen. She tried to think of a tactful way to decline, but he was already adjusting the straps on her diving vest.

"I've got this great new dive computer. State of the art. Cost me eight hundred bucks."

He let go of her strap and turned his attention to one of his own straps, unhooking something. In the dim light she could see a panel glow green. He was pressing buttons on an instrument the size of a large cell phone. Transferring the instrument to his left hand, he stuck out his right hand to shake hers.

"Name's Chuck Crowley. I'm here for the TurboSoft meeting."

Like she was supposed to know what that was.

"I'm Zeph Meyer," she replied reluctantly.

"Well, Zeph, you're in luck tonight. I'm an old hand at this dive thing. Been diving all over the world, Tahiti, The Caymans, all conditions. Just stick close to me and I'll make sure nothing bites that cute little butt of yours."

Was this guy for real? Zephyr choked back a laugh and turned it into a cough, trusting that the darkness hid her annoyance. Hey, apparently she needed a partner. What did it matter? After tonight she'd never see him again, anyway.

"My 'butt' and I thank you in advance."

"Atta girl, Zeph. You're awful small to carry these big tanks. I'll help you get into the water."

"I'm stronger than I look," she responded trying not to sound as defensive as she felt, "I spent most of my childhood on a sailboat."

"No kidding! Well, Zeph, it's a good thing you've had ocean experience. Gonna be damned rough when we jump in."

Jump in. Zephyr repressed a shudder. A sharp gust of wind whipped a lose strand of her hair across her eyes. She tucked it firmly back into her ponytail. No way was this guy going to find out how scared she really was.

`"Oh, sure. Lots." She could have added "in a swimming pool—with the lights on," but she didn't. She hadn't answered any questions honestly since she registered at the Old Hawaii Inn two hours ago. Why start now with this irritating stranger?

Abruptly, the sound of the engines ceased and the boat, sinking down into the waves, began to toss so sharply that she was thrown against Chuck's beefy arm. Before he could wrap it around her shoulders, she shifted quickly away.

"Okay, folks, now listen up." Rip's deep, strong voice caused all heads to turn and face in his direction. He stood in the middle of the deck, leaning against a large, water filled barrel. "Like Jackie explained back at the shop, you're going into a cave tonight because it's where the turtles sleep. And you all came to see the giant turtles, right?"

There was a general murmur of enthusiasm. He continued.

"Actually, the cave is just the beginning of a lava tube that goes for maybe half a mile up to a remote part of the island. You *don't* want to go in there and get lost or stuck, so stay with the group. Understood?"

Heads nodded.

Rip dipped his dive mask into the water, swished it around then lifted it out. "You will bring your masks up to the barrel, rinse them, and then put them on with the strap around your neck. When you and your dive buddy are ready, pick up your fins and move to the back step. I'll be there to help you with your last minute gear check. Jackie will go first as leader, I'll follow along behind. When everyone is down and settled, I'll come back up and stay with the boat."

The tall woman who he had earlier introduced as his partner, flipped her long blond braid over one shoulder and strode across the rocking deck to the swim step at the back of the boat.

"Now remember the signals for night diving," Rip continued, "Make a circle with your light if you are okay.

Waggle your light rapidly back in forth in front of you if you're in trouble. Of course," he added with a confident grin, "You aren't going to *be* in trouble because Jackie and I will be here to take good care of you. Have a great dive."

"Okay, Honey, this is it." Chuck stood up just as a wave hit the boat dumping him back onto the bench.

Zephyr started to take a deep breath, but the wetsuit, clearly not designed to accommodate breasts, refused to allow it. She stood up and moved toward the barrel. *Still had the sea legs at least.* The thought gave her confidence.

She dipped her mask in the water then tried to spit into it the way Kevin had taught her, to keep it from fogging up. But something was wrong. She sucked hard on her tongue. No liquid. Nothing.

"Here, try this." Rip held out a little bottle of mask cleaner. She took it without looking at him.

"Thanks." *No spit. That's a dead giveaway Now he knows how scared I am*, she thought.

"Listen," He leaned conspiratorially close to her ear. "I see you're partnering up with Chuck over there, so pretend you're having a problem with your gear and wait until the other groups have gone so you guys can be last, just in front of me."

So he'd found her out! Somehow he'd discovered her real purpose and now he would keep her from taking the pictures she was sent to--

But Rip continued to speak, his breath warm against her cheek. "I need to keep an eye on him. Any time I see an out of shape guy with brand new, expensive equipment, I know he's going to get into trouble. So stick close to me, okay?"

His voice was kind and held a touch of humor. She looked up at him and, in the dim light, was positive she'd seen him wink. Suddenly she realized she was shaking for reasons having nothing to do with the chill of the night air.

After the other divers were gone, swallowed up by the black water, Zephyr found herself struggling to keep her balance on the heaving platform just below the stern of the boat. The metal air tank strapped to her back, seemed impossibly heavy. The water looked as opaque as a vat of melted tar. Her stomach churned. Blasted airline pretzels. *Please God, don't let me throw up!*

"Get going, Honey! Haven't got all night!" Chuck's voice prodded her from the deck above.

Rip's's strong hand gripped her shoulder. "Take one big step off the boat, then when you come back up to the surface, I'll hand your camera to you."

Unable to speak with the mouthpiece gripped between her teeth, she nodded and, for the moment, shame blotted out fear. If he only knew he was handing her the means to report him to the authorities …

She stuck one fin clad foot into the void and suddenly darkness and churning water surrounded her.

When you come to the surface… But where *was* the surface? All was disorienting darkness. The darkest dark she'd ever *not* seen. Cold water began to work its way into her wetsuit, seeping up from the cuffs and down from her neck.

"That's why they call it a wetsuit, Babe. Your own body heat has to warm the water. Now follow your air bubbles to the surface,

air always rises." Kevin's voice seemed to fill her ears which were already aching from the pressure.

In front of her mask appeared a trail of bubbles. She kicked hard and followed them to the surface, reaching up to receive the camera from Rip's outstretched hand.

"Okay, great!" He shouted over the sound of the wind, "Now swim for the prow, go down the anchor line and wait on the bottom."

The boat loomed menacingly above her. Far from the safe shelter that it had seemed while she was on board, it was now a huge dark shape leaping up and down in time with the waves. It seemed to be trying to devour her. She turned her face away then realized, to her amazement, that safety lay in the calm water below the surface. She began to swim forward and down. Gone was the oppressive weight of the tank. Buoyant salt water was supporting it.

The rope that connected the boat to the anchor felt rough, but reassuringly solid. She began to pull herself down, hand over hand, into the depths. It was like climbing a rope only in reverse. With every handhold she moved deeper into darkness. Even through her wetsuit, she could feel the water growing colder.

Her ears started to hurt like they had at the bottom of the pool, but then she remembered to hold her nose shut and blow like Kevin had taught her. She heard a satisfying *snap* and the pain stopped.

Her heart began to race as she continued her descent. Everything in her cried out *let go of the rope! Swim up towards the air!*

No way. She hadn't come this far to wimp out. Besides, she had to show those macho guys — especially that captain. Why did he have to be so attractive? Why couldn't he look like the craggy-faced captain in *Jaws*?

With a jolt, she landed on solid ground remembering to fold her knees under her so as to not damage any coral. The bottom of the ocean was rocky. Her knees felt the rocks before the tiny beam of her flashlight could pick them out, forty feet below the surface. She directed her light around her in an arc. As her eyes became accustomed to the darkness, she saw to her horror, emerging from under a rock, a wide open mouth filled with sharply pointed teeth. A scream stuck in her throat. Quickly, she remembered that if she opened her mouth her regulator would float away and then she'd loose her air supply.

She willed her breathing to slow down. Just a moray eel. She remembered from years ago that they breathe through their mouths. It wasn't threatening her, just gulping deep breaths to calm its own fear. After all, she'd just dropped down here in the midst of its home like an alien from outer space. The serpent was more startled than she was.

Like a candle in a dark cathedral, her light was only capable of illuminating a small patch of jumbled rock and coral. In spite of her terror, she was thrilled and fascinated with this magical new world. So this was the bottom of the ocean! It could have been the far side of the moon it was so strange. Tiny, red faces of squirrel fish stared at her from under a rock ledge and shot away when she reached toward them.

Suddenly, she felt turbulence in the water. Something big was coming! Shark? Whale? No, just Chuck. He was flailing beside her, his light making a frantic zig zag pattern. *Waggle your light if you're in trouble . . .* He must be in trouble! So now what was she supposed to do? What *could* she do? Dive partners were supposed to take care of each other, but he outweighed her by at least a hundred pounds.

Then another shape appeared beside him. *Rip. Thank God!* She could see his blurry outline fixing something on Chuck's tank and the waggling light became a steady beam. With a quick, graceful kick of his fins, Rip swam past her on his way back to stay with the boat. He flashed the "okay" hand sign, thumb and forefinger pinched, in her direction, then slowed and waited for her to return it to show that she was okay. She hesitated for only a moment then answered, signaling that, to her surprise, she really *was* okay. Her fear was gone.

Well, this is actually fun, she thought. So much more interesting than the swimming pool! She kicked herself up off the bottom and followed Chuck's moving fins, just barely visible in front of her. Her camera, dangling from its strap on her left wrist, bumped against her arm as she pressed through the black water, flashlight in hand.

But the small light beam was like a match in a mineshaft. She thought about all the dark around her. Dark stretching all the way from the North Pole to the South Pole. Nothing but dark water. Well, almost nothing. Her mind flashed back to the South Pacific Islands. After a while you could get really bored with sand and coconut palms, but her father was an oceanographer in love with his work and as long as he had that, he was happy.

The group swam on for what seemed like a very long time with nothing to see except an occasional startled fish. The lights of the lead pair which had been only tiny specks in the distance grew larger. Suddenly Zephyr became aware that the other divers were close around her. Someone shone a light beam upward. It illuminated a rocky ceiling. This was it. They were in the turtle cave. Her throat went tight with terror.

Above her was not air, but solid rock.

No use panicking. I can't find my way out alone anyhow. Calm down! Breathe slowly! The memory of another cave, years ago and far from here, rose up and threatened to choke her. She couldn't give in to it. She'd been only a kid then. Now she was a grown up with a job to do. An important job.

Yanking on her camera strap, she brought the camera up into position.

She didn't have long to wait. In a moment a huge shadow loomed over them. As all flashlight beams converged, the enormous body of a giant sea turtle became visible. On its back, long braid flying out behind her, lay Jackie clutching the front of the animal's shell and looking like something in a cartoon fantasy. Only it *wasn't* a cartoon turtle being ridden, it was a living creature and one of an endangered species.

Zephyr tapped her camera and tapped again catching this illegal act. In her mind she could see her pictures on the pages of *Ocean Observers* magazine. She could imagine the caption now -- *"A sleeping sea turtle requires very little oxygen, but awakened without warning by this irresponsible diver, its respiration rate climbs so quickly that it could actually drown."*

The turtle vanished into the dark. Jackie motioned to the group to follow her deeper into the cave. Her light shown on the huge bodies of more sleeping turtles and at her signal, several of the other divers jumped onto them. The turtles' feet scrabbled wildly as Zephyr's camera clicked. These were the pictures she needed, but the violation of these dignified animals was almost more than she could endure. She was thankful when the last of them vanished and Jackie led the divers out of the cave.

Now that her purpose had been accomplished and the camera swinging from her wrist held the evidence she'd been sent to collect, Zephyr became aware that the water was indeed, colder than she'd expected. She began to shiver. How much further back to the boat? Then she remembered Chuck. A diver always takes care of her buddy, even if he is a jerk. So where was he anyway?

She turned, searching with the flashlight as she did and sure enough, there he was behind her, flashlight waggling side to side again. *Now what?* Reluctantly, she turned and swam back to him. If they didn't hurry, they'd get lost from the group. The very idea caused little jolts of terror to flash down her arms and legs making them feel weak and uncoordinated. Still, dive partners had to stay together. Kevin had taught her that.

Chuck's eyes, in the glow of her flashlight, were wild. He shone his light onto his air gauge and she saw the reason for his panic. Less than 500 pounds of air pressure left. Not enough to make it back to the boat under water. They'd have to go up to the surface and swim. That is if she could remember where "up" was.

With her thumb she indicated "up." He nodded frantically and grabbed her hand. *Follow your bubbles*. It was easier
to follow Chuck's. Huge streams of bubbles were coming
from him. They began to swim for the surface, faster she
feared, than was safe.

As they burst into the air, Zephyr was surprised how
much lighter the night seemed than on the trip out. A gib-
bous moon was playing hide and seek with the clouds. In
the distance she could see the blessed lights of the boat
bobbing up and down. She was a strong swimmer, but the
air tank pressed her down as a wave slapped her in the face.

"Help!" Chuck sputtered. His words sounded like
gargling as he flailed towards her. "Quick! Gimmie your
regulator. I'm out of air. Buddy breathe!"

She spat out her mouthpiece. "Use your snorkel," she
gasped. Salt water scalded her throat leaving its harsh,
briny taste in her mouth.

On the surface, in the wind and rain, the wetsuit
was no help at all. Rip was right, darn it! Her suit wasn't
heavy enough for winter. Her chest felt solid, like trying
to breathe with the rigid chest of a doll. She was shivering more violently now, so that when Chuck grabbed her
mouthpiece away and stuck it in his own mouth, she didn't
have the strength to resist. Oh, let him have it, she thought,
reaching for her snorkel.

But with the short hose attached to her tank, swimming wasn't easy. His weight kept dragging her under the
waves. As she struggled toward the surface, she felt a sudden blow on her forehead. Her mask, wrenched loose by
Chuck's wildly flailing arm, jolted away from her face. Salt

burned her eyes. *Hang onto your mask, Babe. Without it you're blind in the water!* Kevin's instructions came back to her. *If your body washes up somewhere without that face mask on, don't expect flowers from me!*

She lunged for her mask, but as she grabbed it her camera strap slid off her wrist. She tried to reach it. The camera floated for a moment as if in slow motion. Moonlight, glinting off the lens, teased her as it winked below the waves. Too late. It was gone. Her evidence, her reason for being out here at all, was gone. Oh damn. Damn. Damn. Damn. She was going to drown and all for nothing. She replaced the mask over her eyes and nose just as Chuck jerked her back toward him and under the water.

Her body fought to curl up, muscles rigid, to hold what little heat she had left. She could no longer feel her fingers. Her legs below the knees seemed not to exist. Waves of chill ran through her and she shook with painful spasms.

Then, before she could quite comprehend what was happening, Rip's strong arm was around her. He was pushing the button on her dive vest to inflate it more, keeping her higher above the black, churning water. With one quick move he jerked the mouthpiece away from Chuck and gave it back to her.

"Here," he said, "Use mine." He gave his own air hose to the thrashing man.

Rip's arm once again slid around her waist, keeping her face above the waves.

"Okay, relax," he said calmly, "I'll get you back to the boat. Both of you start kicking toward the light over there. That's the *Ipo Nui,* our boat. Jackie is back at the boat with the other divers. She'll be looking for us." He waved his light back and forth toward the distant craft.

Zeph felt something sticky and warm in her mouth. Blood. "I think I'm bleeding,"

Chuck spat the air hose out of his mouth and shouted, "Bleeding? That's gonna attract sharks!"

"Take it easy." Rip's voice was reassuring. "I've never lost a diver to sharks, and I don't intend to start now. Insurance premiums would go through the roof."

The sudden deep roar of *Ipo Nui's* twin diesels drifted across the water. "They're leaving us out here!" Chuck yelled.

"Nonsense." Rip rolled onto his back, holding the violently shivering Zephyr against him. "Jackie spotted my distress signal and she's coming to pick us up. You can quit kicking now. Just relax, both of you."

Zephyr couldn't relax. She was too cold, and too aware of the strong arm still firmly locked around her waist, the comforting shoulder behind her.

"You're okay." Rip's voice was steady despite the lashing of the waves. "You did great. This was just a bad night to be out. Come with us next week and I promise you a better dive. You can have a freebee, on me."

She tried to speak, but all that came from her mouth was a bubbly sound.

Then the huge, dark bulk of the boat blotted out the wild sky. She heard a jumble of voices. Strong hands dragged them on board.

One pair of hands took Zephyr's fins while others removed her vest and tank. She didn't really care what they did. The shivering had stopped and in its place she felt a powerful sleepiness. Everything seemed very far away and dreamlike even as someone peeled off her wetsuit.

She had the sense of being carried down steps to an inside cabin. Soothing hands were bandaging her forehead and removing her swimming suit. Zephyr thought she should protest, but when she tried to speak, the only sound that she could make was the chattering of her teeth. She felt herself being placed on a bunk. Rough blankets wrapped her naked body then something else...the bare chest of a man was pressed against her. His soft chest hair warmed her nipples, erect from the cold.

"You're okay now. I'm just warming you up. Even mild hypothermia is nothing to fool with."

The voice, deep and rich, was Rip's and the hard bicep against her cheek was his also. Cold and exhausted as she was, the irony did not escape her. She was naked in the arms of the man she had been sent to penalize, and what's more, she was enjoying it!

2

"Don't get alarmed. This isn't rape or even sexual harassment. You needn't bother to thank me now, but I'm saving your life."

"I don't...need...saving..." Zephyr whispered drowsily, wondering what on earth he could be talking about.

"You're hypothermic. Cold, in other words." His voice sounded matter-of-fact, professional. A strange contrast to their position, she thought, through the mental fog that had closed in on her. The cut on her forehead burned.

"B-But -- I"

"Shhh, don't try to talk. I'm not taking advantage of you. This is standard emergency procedure. If we had hot water on board I could have substituted hot water bottles for my body heat, but unfortunately your buddy Chuck used it all for his shower while we were attending to you. Now we haven't got hot water, so you're stuck with me for a while."

She felt him gently press her wrist in his big fingers.

"I'm...f-f-fi-ne. Slowly she became aware of the soft fabric of his cotton shorts. Apparently she was the only one who was naked.

"Quiet. I'm taking your pulse. I need to count."

With the arm that was under her, he pressed her closer. She could smell the rich warmth of him through the rubbery scent left by his wetsuit. Without warning or conscious thought, a flash of lust raced across her body.

No! What am I thinking?

"G-Give m-me my c-clo—" Her voice came out in little gasps.

"Like I said, don't try to talk. Save your energy."

"I w-want m-my c-c-clozz—"

"Shhh." His finger pressed lightly against her lips. "I'm going to resist the temptation to say 'I told you so,' but I seem to remember saying something about hypothermia being serious *before* you got yourself into this."

Indignation gave strength to her weakened muscles as she struggled to sit up.

"Hey, take it easy." His arms tightened around her with the same steely strength that had felt so reassuring out in the dark ocean. "You need to rest. I don't want to scare you, but if we don't get you warmed up, you could experience a fatal heart arrhythmia before we can get you some medical attention."

Reluctantly, she surrendered to his firm embrace. "I-I'm...not...c-cold...just s-sleepy."

"Right. Denial and sleepiness are two of the defining symptoms of hypothermia. Now just relax and think warm thoughts."

Exactly the problem, she realized. Lying here, in the arms of this disconcerting stranger, her thoughts and her body *were* reacting warmly. Much *too* warmly for a woman who was engaged to be married in a few months.

"I—I'm going…to…m-married…s-soon."

"Congratulations," he said flatly, but not unkindly. "I saw your ring. All the more reason to concentrate on staying alive."

"Can't…you j-just get me a hot d-drink?" To her relief, her voice was beginning to sound less wobbly. The treatment, though weird, did seem to be working.

"Nope. Definitely not. That's how they used to treat hypothermia until someone realized that warming too fast brought on shock. Tell me, not to change the subject or anything, but why didn't you wait until your honeymoon to take a trip to these romantic isles?"

He rolled the "r" on romantic so grandly that she found herself smiling even as her befogged brain struggled frantically to think up a plausible answer to his question. Why? Why, indeed? Anything but the real reason.

"I just…"

"Just what?" His voice was gentle, encouraging. It made her feel like telling him everything – her fight with Kevin, even the sea turtles…if only she weren't so darn sleepy…

"Just needed…needed…a-a… change."

"Oh, yeah? So soon? Never mind… None of my business. Forget I asked."

Worn out by the effort of inventing another lie, Zephyr relaxed against the warmth of his body and dozed. The motion of the boat pressed them together with the rhythm of the waves.

■ ■ ■

She had no way of judging how long she'd slept before she was awakened by a woman's sharp voice. For a moment she couldn't remember where she was or to whom the broad chest pressed against her belonged. Kevin? No. Too big. Certainly not Kevin.

"Shhh. Calm down, Jackie. You know I'm not doing this for fun."

"Sure. I know. Tough job but somebody has to make the sacrifice, right?"

"You're down here so who's at the helm?" Rip's voice was soft, but with a barely perceptible edge.

"I set the autopilot."

"Well, get back up there. We've got passengers we're responsible for. What if we hit something?"

"Now you're giving orders? I thought we were partners."

"We are, but right now I'm the captain. We'll be at the harbor soon and there'll be traffic. You need to get back on the bridge."

"Yeah, well you'd better get *her* dressed before she starts yelling for a lawyer!"

"Right, but don't forget —"

"Forget what?"

"You owe me two beers."

Zephyr jumped at the sound of a door slamming.

"Are you okay?" His voice was suddenly gentle again.

"Yes. I'm getting up now!"

"No, you aren't." he said, wrapping the blanket over her breasts as he moved away. "We've alerted the paramedics by radio. They'll bring a stretcher in and take you to the hospital for observation.

"Forget it! I don't need all that! Just a cup of coffee and I'll be fine!"

Rip tucked the blankets tightly around her and climbed out of the bunk. Standing, he leaned over her. A dimple flashed in the left side of his face as he smiled.

"You *are* a tough one, aren't you?"

■ ■ ■

But she didn't feel very tough the next morning. Stepping out of the dark lobby of the small community hospital, Zephyr blinked in the glare of the mid-morning sunlight. The humid air was all over her like a huge, soggy animal. How could it have been so cold last...*was* it really just last night?

She tried to sort through her memories and place them in some kind of order. Siren. Faces inside the ambulance floating over her like balloons. Voices. A man's voice. Was he talking to her? "M'am do you know where you are? What is the date today?"

Why was he asking such stupid questions? Of course she knew the date, if they'd just give her a minute to think.

A woman's voice—"ETA thirty minutes. Twenty-two -year-old female scuba diver. Possible hypothermia. Slight contusion on forehead..."

Female scuba diver? Were they talking about her?

Bright lights. Something squeezing on her arm. They were pasting little things on to her. More voices. "BP one-ten over sixty." And then a strange, long night of delicious sleep interrupted all too often by an inflating blood pressure cuff and cheerful voices asking more silly questions.

Finally this morning a young Asian doctor patted her shoulder, placing a prescription in her hand as he pronounced her well enough to leave the hospital.

So now what? Where was she anyhow? Wailuku Community Hospital? But where was Wailuku? Where was the Old Hawaii Inn and her suitcase? Above all, *where were her clothes?* Finding no "personal belongings" bag for her, the friendly blond nurse had given her a shapeless muu-muu to wear. It was covered with hideous yellow and purple flowers. Her reflection, vague in the glass door as she stepped outside, was almost enough to send her into a relapse. Good thing she wasn't connected to that heart monitor anymore! She stood still for a moment, not having a clue which way to go. This certainly wasn't Lahaina. Then she heard a familiar voice behind her.

Rip.

"Hey lady! Need a ride?"

How could she face him now, after last night? Without turning around, she started walking away from the hospital along the curving, one way drive. "I hope you know where you're going."

Almost against her will, she glanced in the direction of the voice." A pair of eyes, fringed in dark lashes, caught hers. It was as if thunder from last night's storm had suddenly returned and burst the sky open.

He must have felt it too. There could be no doubt about that. Something crackled through the damp air between them. It was as real as the white Wrangler in which he sat.

Rip grinned and a dimple in his left cheek danced. "I figured you wouldn't remember much about how you got here." His left arm, bicep flattened against the bottom of the open window, was the same arm that had held her last night. Held her naked against him. For a moment she couldn't speak.

"Can I give you a ride back to your hotel?"

Why was he here? What sort of follow-up was he expecting after last night's weird intimacy? Her face felt painfully hot. She wanted to hide.

"No, thank you."

Looking straight down the sidewalk, she started to walk briskly. Or at least as briskly as possible in the rubber sandals the hospital had given her. They made flopping noises that undercut the air of dignity she was trying to project.

"Where are you staying?"

The Wrangler tires crunched beside her, next to the curb. She was seized by a desperate desire to run. But where? She had no idea where she was. Besides, the thought suddenly hit her, she'd lost her camera-- her evidence. She still had the assignment to complete. Better be polite to him, at least for now.

She turned. "Lahaina. Old Hawaii Inn." She fixed her gaze on a waving palm tree at the end of the block. Anything to avoid meeting his eyes.

"Well, you're walking in the wrong direction. And, by the way, it's about twenty-five miles. Hope those shoes hold up."

Twenty-five miles! And she was tired already. Reluctantly, she turned to face him and felt that unsettling jolt again. So she hadn't imagined it. What *was* that peculiar sensation?

"I guess I don't have much choice, do I?"

"You could take a taxi. Of course you'd have to take out a bank loan to pay the driver. Or maybe you could use some of the charm that attracted Chuck?"

"Oh puh - *leeze*!" She laughed and felt her shoulders relax.

"Hey, I'm sorry," he said. His expression turning concerned. "I shouldn't tease someone who just got out of the hospital. And someone who just got out of the hospital shouldn't be walking twenty-five miles. Come on. Get in. I promise I'll be a perfect gentleman." He leaned across the seat and opened the door.

Zephyr hesitated, then wrapping the muu-muu tightly against herself, she hurried around the back of the vehicle and climbed into the passenger seat. Somehow dignity seemed to demand that she hide those huge flowers as much as possible. She hitched the extra fabric under her.

"Well, okay. Thanks. I need to get back to my own clothes before the Fashion Police catch me."

He laughed. She tried not to notice again the dimple that flashed in his cheek or the way his eyes crinkled at the corners. It was the first time she'd seen him in daylight. Did he *have* to be so darn good looking? For some silly reason this made last night even more embarrassing. *Think about Kevin. Think about Kevin.*

Rip handed her the seatbelt buckle. "Don't worry about the Fashion Police. Here on Maui they actually enforce the wearing of purple and yellow flowers."

In spite of herself, she smiled. *Think about the sea turtles. The sea turtles.*

"Oh. Well, I guess that explains what happened at the airport yesterday afternoon. I had to hide in the ladies room until that girl who was determined to put flowers around my neck disappeared."

He gave her a quick look before pulling away from the curb.

"I remember that you just got here yesterday. From where?"

"Phoenix."

"So. That explains a lot." Rip nodded as he turned the Wrangler away from the hospital and onto a highway.

"A lot of what?"

"A lot of why you were so sensitive to the cold."

"I wasn't sensitive! I was just--"

"I'm sorry. I didn't mean you weren't a genuine macho diver. I was speaking from a medical perspective. Jackie should have asked if you'd had time to rest from your flight before she signed you up."

Zephyr gazed out across the bright green sugar cane fields. Tall, grassy stalks waved in the wind.

"Maybe she did. I can't remember." She'd been so nervous when she booked the dive, she'd probably have lied if Jackie had asked if she was a mammal.

"Nice of you to cover for her, but if she didn't ask she should have. A second Rule Number One: Be sure your divers are rested and sober. How much did you have to drink on the plane?"

Zeph felt her face go hot again.

"I wasn't drunk!"

"I didn't say you were. If I'd smelled booze on your breath I'd have very politely asked you to go back to your hotel, sleep it off, and come back tomorrow."

"Then why did you ask how much I'd had to drink?"

"Because alcohol also makes your body less resistant to cold. Booze plus fatigue equals you in the hospital."

And naked in your arms. NO! Don't think about it.

"Okay, I had a couple glasses of wine. I'm a nervous flier and we were in the air for six hours."

And I was trying to forget that fight with Kevin.

"So add the emotional stress of flying and the picture gets even clearer." He turned his attention away from the road, which was now running alarmingly high above the water, and focused hard on her.

"Tell the truth now. Exactly how much ocean diving have you done?"

His eyes were an amazing blue-green. The color of the lagoon she glimpsed beyond his shoulder.

"Hadn't you better concentrate on the road?"

"I don't have to. I could drive it in my sleep. Now answer the question."

They both stared through the windshield for a long minute. Zephyr sighed deeply. "None, "she whispered.

"What?"

He was looking at her again. She could see his shocked expression out of the corner of her eye though she continued to stare straight ahead.

"I said--" She cleared her throat. "I said, 'none.' As in 'not any.' As in 'never.' Okay?"

"NO! It is damn well not 'okay!'"

The Wrangler veered to the right and they were quite suddenly bouncing along the shoulder on the right hand side of the road, coming to a stop at the base of a rocky cliff.

He grabbed her shoulders in both of his hands and turned her to face him. Automatically, she flinched, braced for an outburst of fury.

It didn't come.

"What were you thinking?" His voice was quiet and hard but somehow more chilling than Kevin's outbursts or even her father's.

"I . . . I don't know. I guess I just thought I knew what I was doing. I used to snorkel and free dive when we lived on our boat. I thought it would be pretty much the same."

"The *same*? Lady, don't you realize there's a *huge* difference? It's like saying roller skating is 'pretty much' like driving a car! Don't you realize you could have gotten yourself killed? Even if you don't care about that, think about poor old Chuck. He may be a jerk, but he's probably got a family somewhere, what right did you have to jeopardize him? Or me, for that matter?"

"I'm sorry." Even to her own ears, that sounded lame.

"So it wasn't enough to just jump in without warning us, you had to start with a night dive in bad weather?"

"I…I thought if I told you, you wouldn't have let me go."

"You're darn right I wouldn't. So where did you pass your certification check out dive, in a lake?"

"No."

"River?"

"Not exactly."

"Look, I'm not in the mood to play twenty questions. I know you have a certificate; I saw the copy of it with your consent form. So where did you do the check- out dive?"

"In a swimming pool. The deep end." She mumbled the words, addressing them to the yellow and purple flowers in her lap.

"What imbecile let you get away with that? He should have his instructors' permit pulled before he kills somebody."

Zeph turned her face toward the window to hide a renegade grin that threatened to turn up one corner of her mouth. What irony! Here I came to turn him in to the authorities and suddenly he's talking about doing the same thing to Kevin

"The 'imbecile' as you call him is my fiancé." Her voice was defiant. She looked straight into his eyes and tried not to notice those thick curly lashes.

For a moment he just stared back at her. Slowly, he put the Wrangler in gear, stepped on the gas and turned back onto the pavement.

■ ■ ■

Rip thought later that there must have been some perfect remark he could have made. Some way he could have shown his utter contempt for the guy, not only as a scuba instructor, but more importantly as a husband-to-be. However even three hours later, lying on his back in his bunk listening to the mooring lines creak in the afternoon swells, he couldn't think of one. Is there a polite way to tell a woman that the jerk she loves has no regard for her safety? Not bloody likely!

Which was too bad because she was a babe. Stubborn perhaps, maybe even a bit pig-headed, but definitely a babe. He'd been hooked by that world class smile that started out shy and ended up dazzling. She was tiny but had plenty of curves in all the right places. He felt a pleasant, warm stirring as he remembered those curves snuggled up against him in this very bunk. The soft breasts, nipples erect from the cold, the taut belly, the small firm buns - barely a handful for him as he'd pulled her against himself, lending his body heat.

Oh, okay. So she might not have been in any really life threatening danger, but what he'd done *was* approved emergency treatment for hypothermia. He could certainly have defended his actions if he'd had to. But he was glad he hadn't had to. Yet.

Was it some need not to risk antagonizing her that had caused him to offer her a free lesson tomorrow? He winced at the idea. He'd never liked to think of himself as a manipulative kind of guy, but in the tourist business you have to please the customer. Make sure you have good word of mouth. Mouth. There it was again, the memory of her mouth sipping iced tea through a straw at lunch.

Lunch had been his idea. He'd walked her into her hotel, of course. Their feet made hollow thumping sounds as they crossed the wide, wooden porch. The red painted boards had endured almost a hundred years of vacationers' sandy feet. It made you forgive the dusty, old-building smell of the lobby.

After the confrontation by the side of the road, neither of them had spoken much the rest of the way into Lahaina. They'd kept the conversation general – the weather, his comments about the scenery, basic tour guide kinds of stuff. Impersonal.

He suddenly realized that he very much didn't want it to end that way.

"Did they feed you the usual gourmet hospital lunch before turning you lose?"

"Lunch? No. There was some kind of gray mushy stuff in a bowl for breakfast. Oatmeal, I think. But I escaped lunch."

"Then perhaps you'd care to join me? The restaurant here is a regular stop on the tour bus route, but the food is pretty good in spite of that."

She looked vaguely uncomfortable for a moment before she answered. Was it what he'd said about her boyfriend? But then she flashed that smile again and nodded.

"Well . . . okay. Thanks."

The bar was adjacent to the lobby, through a swinging "old west" half-door. Like the rest of the hotel, it was "authentic old.' The only attempt at climate control consisted of wooden fans suspended from the high ceiling. There was an outside area for dining, but a tour bus had recently disgorged a group of Asian tourists so the only seating available was in the bar. They found a table next to the window which had a nice view of the harbor.

He pulled her chair out for her. As she sat down, her soft hair brushed the back of his hand. He remembered the feel of that hair, damp then, against his chest in the bunk. The memory was so intense that he had to sit down.

"So . . . " He spoke quickly in order to redirect his thoughts to something more professional. " . . . so would it be too nosy to ask *why* this guy who supposedly has your best interests at heart, gave you an Open Water Scuba Certificate when you never got out of the swimming pool?"

She looked down at her lap again, then suddenly stood up.

"You know what . . . I need to get into some clothes of my own. If you don't mind, just order me some iced tea and a small salad. I'll be right back."

He watched her dart through the swinging doors. Graceful. He'd noticed that about her last night even on the lurching boat. Seemed used to the motion of the sea. Then why . . . ?

Never mind. In the two years he and Jackie had been running the dive boat, he'd given up trying to guess why people on vacation did any of the stupid things they did. Maybe it had been a mistake to dump a cushy paralegal job with his ex-father-in-law's law firm in L.A. Maybe he could have gotten used to wearing a suit and working in an office building where none of the windows opened even a crack. Maybe.

He gazed out at the boats bobbing on their moorings --
one in particular. His boat, the *Ipo Nui*. She looked beautiful:
sleek and white. She was worth every moment of the time
he'd spent under water scraping the crud off the bottom of
other people's boats. He'd worked such long hours that he'd
developed chronic ear infections. Even at that, he never could
have started his own dive shop if it hadn't been for Jackie.
Jackie. Now there was another problem . . . Forget it. Think
about it later.

But later he was thinking about Zephyr. He watched
her soft lips pressed against her straw as she sipped her ice
tea. When she looked at him, he noticed for the first time
the color of her eyes. Golden. He'd never seen eyes like
that before. They were kind of brown and kind of green,
but the net impression was golden. Rip drew a deep, calming breath before he spoke.

"When you rushed off to rid yourself of our local cos-
tume, in the process offending all of us who consider ourselves Hawaiians, you were about to tell me why the guy
you are planning to marry didn't insist you actually *have*
open water experience before giving you an Open Water
certificate."

"Yes, I know." Her fork stalled in midair. She laid it
carefully back on her salad plate. "It's a long story."

"I'm in no hurry."

"Okay, but remember I warned you." She carefully
folded an edge of the paper napkin that sat under her glass,
pressing hard on it as if to keep it from flying away. "This
may be more than you want to know about me."

"If it is, I'll let you know," he said.

"My mother died last month."

"I'm sorry." His voice was sympathetic.

"Yes, well she'd been sick a long time." Zephyr looked out of the window, avoiding his eyes. "I took care of her because I was the only person she trusted."

"Trusted?"

"Not to look at her with . . . um. . .shock – or pity. She had melanoma. The surgery, the radiation . . . well . . . she couldn't bear to look in a mirror."

Outside a tour bus wheezed and belched diesel fumes. Rip saw Zephyr's lower lip quiver and was glad that the noise from the bus had given her a moment to regain her composure.

"I think I understand," he said.

"No. No, you can't possibly . . . " She gazed out the window as if she'd been speaking only to herself. "I don't mean to be rude, but my family was . . . well, different."

"Different? In what way?" He studied her face, intrigued.

"I . . . we . . . " she began, then stopped aiming the full force of those golden eyes at him. Her voice dropped to little more than a whisper. "I don't know why I'm telling you this. I don't usually talk to strangers this way."

"Strangers? After last night do I still qualify as a stranger?" He had been trying for a light tone, hoping to relax her and make her smile. Immediately, he regretted it.

"Mr. MacKinsey . . . " her soft lips went suddenly tight. "Need I remind you that I was not exactly a willing participant?" She sat up very straight. For a moment he was afraid she would walk out and leave him alone there. Alone with two salads.

"No, of course not," he said quickly, hoping he looked convincingly ashamed. "I'm sorry. That was an inappropriate thing for me to say. But please call me Rip. When someone says, 'Mr. MacKinsey', I think they are talking about my father."

She relaxed a little and almost smiled. "Okay . . . Rip. I guess I should be grateful--"

"Hey, forget it." Now it was his turn to be embarrassed. He changed the subject. "I'm still waiting to hear about your 'different' family."

She gave him a wan smile. "Okay, well . . . My grandfather died when I was ten. My father inherited enough money to quit his university job, teaching oceanography, and buy a boat so he could actually *practice* oceanography. That was his dream. He wanted to study the migration patterns of air breathing sea life and, in the process, sail around the world."

Rip leaned forward and gave a long, low whistle. "All the way around?"

"Well, no. Only half. We spent five years in the South Pacific."

"Didn't you have to go to school?"

She looked back at him with a slightly teasing smile. "My father was a teacher, remember?"

"Oh, sure. Sorry."

"When I went to live with my aunt so I could go to a regular high school, I was actually ahead of the other kids, academically at least."

"Did they finally give up on the sea fairing life?"

"My mother did. After her first operation. She was a redhead and the sun must have been too much for her skin. She blamed my father and his love of the ocean, so she left him, took me and moved to Phoenix. The desert was as far from water as she could imagine. She only went outdoors at night and she said she never wanted to see the ocean again."

"And your father stayed on the boat while you got the job of taking care of your mother."

She nodded. Rip noticed she'd stopped even pretending to eat her salad.

"That must have been rough."

"It was. That's why when I saw Kevin's ad in the newspaper, I thought scuba lessons might be just what I needed. I'd been swimming laps every day for exercise, but that got boring."

He nodded. So she had a low tolerance for boredom, too.

"The problem was that after the cancer came back, I couldn't leave Mom for more than an hour or two at a time. Kevin was willing to come to our house and give me lessons in our pool, but when it came time for me to go with his regular class to do their check out dives off Baja, I couldn't go."

"And Kevin signed off on the certificate anyhow?"

"Yes. At the time he didn't think I'd ever use it."

"Why did you? And why a night dive?"

Zephyr's face turned suddenly pink as she tipped her chin upwards into the breeze from the whirling ceiling fan. She glanced quickly around the room. Her eyes drew Rip's attention once again. A remarkable shade of golden brown. Had he ever seen eyes that color before? And why was she blinking so rapidly? He was at the point of asking her if she had something in her eye when she focused on the life-size carved wooden figure suspended over the bar.

"Is that a figurehead from an old ship?"

"That's what they say."

"The poor lady looks positively catatonic."

"Seems to me she looks pretty good for being 150 years old, give or take a decade."

"Really. What were sailing ships doing way out here so long ago?"

"Slaughtering whales." Seeing the look of pain on Zephyr's face, Rip regretted the harshness of his words. There wasn't any nice way to say it, though. Can't change the facts.

"No wonder her face is so sad," Zephyr said. "Just think of what she must have seen."

"I try not to."

"The harpoons on the wall look really scary."

"It was a scary business, for the sailors as well as the whales."

"Life is scary. I guess that's why I like turtles. They can just pull their heads in and ignore it."

Thinking about it now, lying on his bunk, he tried to make sense of her response. Had he gotten too personal too soon?

"I'm really tired," she'd said. "Thanks for lunch and for the ride. And I suppose I should thank you for the body heat although they didn't seem all that concerned about me at the hospital. I have only your word that your 'treatment' was necessary."

She stood up and was about to leave when he'd made the offer about the free lesson. He'd actually been surprised when, after a moment when she seemed to be considering something, she'd accepted. They agreed on tomorrow afternoon, after the regular morning group (the paying customers!) finished.

Now to tell Jackie that she'd be minding the shop alone.

3

"Good afternoon. *Ocean Observers.* This is Angie. How can I help you?"

"Hi, Angie. This is Zephyr Meyers. I'm working on the sea turtle investigation in Hawaii."

"Oh, yes. You're the one who wrote some background articles for us. I've been meaning to call and thank you. "

"Thanks, but you needn't." Zephyr realized her hands were sweating when she almost fumbled her phone onto the floor. She quickly changed it to her left hand and continued. "It was just library research and some things I remembered from sailing years ago."

"Hey, don't knock it. What you wrote was good. So what's happening?"

"Ummm, well unfortunately nothing right now. I did a dive last night with Mid-Pacific Diving, and I got a photos of one of the owners and some tourists riding sea turtles, just like the anonymous letter you got said."

"Those jerks! No wonder the green sea turtle is endangered."

"Yes, but --"

"So what's the problem? Sounds like you got the goods on them."

"Well I did, but --" Zephyr set the phone down and wiped her damp right hand on her shorts, then picked the phone back up again. "-- the thing is, I lost the camera with the pictures in it."

"Oh, rats. Too bad. Sorry about your camera. Can you buy another one and arrange to go out again?"

"Well I can, yes, but they won't be doing another night dive for a week."

"Whew. Another week in Paradise. What a bummer! Listen, where are you staying? Okay if I call you on this number? Is it your cell phone?"

"Yes. If I'm out on the water just leave a message and I'll call you back. I'm staying at the Old Hawaii Inn."

"Cool. I hope it isn't too expensive. But if you need financial help with the hotel bill . . . maybe we can --"

"No. That's not a problem. I just wanted to let you know why I'm going to miss the deadline. Gwen wanted it for the Hawaiian sea turtle feature in the next issue."

"No big deal. We'll use it as a follow-up. Keeps the focus on irresponsible ecotourism for another month."

"Tell Gwen I'm sorry."

"Sure. No problem. Just your normal Murphy's Law kind of thing. How did you happen to lose it anyway? Are you okay?"

For just an instant Zephyr struggled with the urge to tell this sympathetic sounding stranger about the cold, the dark, the wind, the rain, the boat captain . . . But the years alone with her parents on the sailboat had taught her to keep her feelings to herself.

"I'm fine. Just clumsy."

They both laughed and concluded the conversation with Zephyr's promise to email the incriminating shots as soon as she had them.

After she disconnected, a tremendous lassitude came over her. Jet lag, the exhausting dive, and whatever they'd given her in the hospital won out over her desire to see more of Maui and she fell into a deep, peaceful, sixteen hour sleep.

■ ■ ■

The next morning, after finishing a delicious breakfast of mangoes, papayas, and fresh pineapple drenched in coconut syrup and topped off by several cups of rich Kona coffee, Zephyr started off down the main street of Lahaina.

This isn't the Hawaii I expected at all, she thought. There were no wide beaches, just a rocky waterfront with buildings perched on stilts above it. The buildings themselves looked more like the Old West than the tropics. They were mostly two story, wooden, with second floor porches cantilevered over the sidewalk. The lower floors were filled with shops selling tee shirts, beach mats, monkeys made out of coconut shells and other assorted tourist goodies. The street glistened with puddles left over from the rain.

Zephyr made her way through a group of elderly couples all of whom were dressed in matching Hawaiian shirts, and stepped inside a camera shop. Fifteen minutes and one credit card transaction later, she came out carrying a small plastic bag. It bumped against her leg as she walked back toward the hotel.

It's only a camera, she reminded herself. But then why did it feel so much like a live bomb?

■ ■ ■

Back in her room, she put on her swimming suit with a white tee shirt and denim shorts over it. Rip would be there to pick her up for her scuba lesson at 12:30. She had just enough time to email Kevin.

Why not call? .

Okay. So she was being cowardly. But if she didn't have to hear the disappointment in his voice, it would be easier to tell him that she was going to be gone longer than the few days she'd planned. She turned off her phone and stuck it in the drawer of the night stand.

Laptop in hand, she stepped out onto a balcony overlooking the courtyard. A raucous squawking issued from the tall, shaggy pandanus leaves that filled most of the area between wings of the building. Large black birds with orange feet were arguing fiercely among themselves. The heavy sweet smell of blossoms seemed to come from everywhere and nowhere. Palm leaves rattled in the wind.

Zephyr felt a sudden, sharp awareness of the fact that she was alone. She tried to think of Kevin, but was shocked to realize that she couldn't summon up his face clearly. Writing to him would help. She sank down onto a white wicker chair, fired up the computer and stared at the blank "new message" page.

> *Hi Kevin,*
> *I need to stay another week. I'm sorry.*

No other words flowed onto the waiting screen. She stared so long that her screen saver came on and she found herself gazing at drifting turtles. Finally she just signed the message and pressed "send." Maybe she'd call him in a few days, when he'd had a chance to cool down.

She struggled again to remember Kevin's face, his voice, but instead her traitor mind kept calling up a picture of flashing dimples, long dark eyelashes, and sea green eyes. It was a picture of the man she was here to damage. It was a picture of Rip.

■ ■ ■

Perhaps it was the memory of that mental picture that caused her face to flush hotly as Rip helped her into the Wrangler two hours later. Perhaps it was the strong, confident way that he touched her elbow. Suddenly she felt as naked as a turtle without a shell.

"Are you all rested up now?" He climbed back into the driver's seat then looked searchingly at her as he turned the key in the ignition. "If you aren't, we can wait a few days."

"No . . . I mean, yes. I'm fine."

"You sure? Let me look at that cut."

He lifted her bangs and checked the cut, now no longer even bandaged.

"Say, you heal fast! Goes with your macho image, I guess."

"Are you making fun of me?"

"Would I do that?" He smiled gently and put the car in gear. When she didn't answer he said, "No, of course I'm not making fun of you. I admire your courage, really I do. I'm sorry for being so harsh yesterday. It's just that it's a big responsibility taking people diving. Sometimes I get a little self-righteous about preparation."

"I understand. I guess I just didn't expect it to be so . . . so . . ."

"Real? That's what people often say. Folks get so used to virtual experience that they think they can do anything even if they've only seen it on TV. Comes as a shock when they get out there and find out what real adventure feels like. As you know, it's not always fun."

"My mother used to say that 'adventure is what you're having when you're wishing you were home.'"

"And your father? What did he say?"

"I don't really remember." Zeph looked out of the window and tried to remember her father. Funny how his voice and face had grown fuzzy just like Kevin's. She let herself be distracted by the scenery. They were out of town now and rolling along a highway that wound between towering green mountains on one side and a tree fringed narrow beach on the other. The water lay still and bright as the surface of a glass topped table.

"Where are we going?" she asked, conscious that she was changing the subject. This too-sexy guy was getting personal enough to make her very uncomfortable.

"Olowalu. That's the General Store up ahead. Our diving spot is just past it. Great fish and turtles."

They drove under a canopy of kiawe trees, past the little wooden store with its saggy front porch, and parked next to the beach.

Rip turned to her and smiled encouragingly.

"You'll love it and it's very safe. We won't be deeper than 30 feet and there's plenty of coral around to stand on if you get tired."

"Stand on!" Forgetting her shyness in the heat of her outrage, she turned to face him. "Do you realize how long it takes coral to grow just one inch? *Centuries* of reef building can be destroyed in the time it take for you to set one of your fins on—"

Rip held up his hand in front of her. "Hey! Hey, take it easy. We're not the first ones here you know. People step on this reef every day—"

"Just because other people do it doesn't make it right. Someone has to take responsibility—"

Rip leaned his left arm across the wheel and turned to face her squarely. "Now wait just one darn minute here. I take plenty of responsibility. I give a lecture to my regular groups every time we go out to Molokini. 'Stay off the coral,' I tell them. It's a living thing . . . And say, just where do you get off, Miss-I-got-certified-in-a-swimming-pool, telling *me* how to run my business?" His tone was light, but those green eyes were suddenly hard in a way she hadn't seen before.

Zephyr took a deep breath. He was right, sort of. She could see people walking on the reef even now. This *was* his turf and he *was* doing her a favor. Probably this wasn't the time or place for an environmental awareness lecture. Besides, if she wasn't careful she could blow her cover as just an ordinary tourist out for fun in the sun.

"I . . . I'm sorry. Sometimes I get too . . . too . . . "

"Passionate?" He inquired with a lifted eyebrow.

"Involved," she finished firmly. "Now hadn't we better get started?"

He shrugged. "If you're sure you're all through with the oceanography lecture."

Zeph could feel anger pounding in her chest, but this time she held it in check. She'd have the last word when the Fish and Game people closed him down. For now, better keep her mouth shut.

They didn't actually walk on the coral, but once in their dive gear they followed the sand channels out between the coral heads. Walking in swim fins was clumsy, so as soon as they were clear of shallow water, they flattened out with their face masks in the water. Rip led the way, looking back frequently to make sure she was still behind him.

Gradually, the water grew deeper and when they had gotten so far from shore that Zeph was afraid to look back, Rip turned and signaled "down" to her with a jerk of his thumb.

Zephyr exhaled deeply as Kevin had taught her, and almost without trying, she sank below the surface and into a magical world of light and color. All around her swam fish in many shapes and sizes, brightly colored beyond belief. There were vivid yellow fish with raccoon-like black masks. There were green ones with blue spots and white ones with black stripes. A school of rounded yellow fish floated motionless, suspended above the white sand. A pale blue fish, tinged with yellow flitted past, his bright pink lips making him look like a clown in make-up. All around them, like some medieval version of Heaven, the sea glowed a luminous vivid blue through which shafts of filtered sunlight glittered and winked.

The scene was so hypnotically beautiful that Zeph forgot for a moment what she was supposed to be doing. Rip's tap on her shoulder brought back her focus and she returned his rounded thumb and forefinger "okay" signal. They settled onto the sandy bottom on their knees, fins tucked beneath them in proper scuba form.

Before they left the beach, Rip had explained that he would be asking her to take off her mask so she could practice putting it back on under water, therefore she wasn't surprised when he took off his mask and signaled her to do the same.

She pulled the strap off the top of her head, untangling her hair from the buckle as she did so. Immediately the beautiful world vanished to be replaced by blurry blue confusion. She bit back a moment of panic. She'd done this before in the pool and up on the surface two nights ago. She could do it now.

Scooping her hair back, she pulled the mask over her face and secured the strap. Pressing hard on the top of the mask above her eyes, she loosened the bottom of the mask just enough so that one hard exhalation through her nose emptied it of water and replaced it with air. She could see again!

In front of her, Rip was nodding approval and shaping his thumb and first finger into the "okay" sign. In spite of herself, she was glad that she had pleased him. After motioning her to follow, Rip turned and kicked toward deeper water. Zephyr swam behind him giving her nose a quick squeeze to equalize the pressure in her ears.

Then she saw them, emerging like a great procession from behind towers of coral -- the sea turtles. They were huge, grand and swift. In spite of their enormous bulk, their strong flippers propelled them with amazing speed and grace. They seemed almost to be flying. Zephyr's heart greeted them like the old friends they were and, as if he somehow received her message, the leader turned his head to look at her.

But where his eyes should have been were only ugly tumors. He was almost blind, propelling himself on instinct alone.

Zeph drew a quick, horrified breath and felt the compressed air fill her lungs. As she watched the other dark shapes soar past, she realized that many of the turtles had lumps like his, some on the flippers, many around the face and eyes. What could have happened? Who or what had done this to those beautiful creatures?

She turned to Rip who was floating beside her. Understanding her distress, he shook his head, then pointed back in the direction from which they had come.

A few minutes later as she peeled off her wetsuit and dropped it onto the beach blanket, Zephyr searched Rip's face for a sign of the same distress she was feeling. To her surprise, she saw it in the clinching of his jaw and the tightness around his mouth.

"The turtles," she said. "What happened to them?"

"Tumors," he answered grimly. "It's caused by a virus. We've been seeing it for years now, but nobody can prove the cause for certain. It's probably the result of pollution from all the big hotels and golf courses. Fertilizer runs off into the ocean and causes growth of an algae the turtles eat. The algae contains the virus."

"Has anyone tried to prove that?"

"A few scientists here at the University of Hawaii and a couple of universities on the Mainland, but no one else seems that interested."

Zephyr almost burst out, "*Ocean Observers* will be interested!" but stopped herself just in time.

Wrapping the towel around her hair, she gazed out at the twinkling water, green over the reef changing abruptly to dark blue nearer the horizon. The ocean: vast, mysterious, but vulnerable. She thought of the terrible sights she'd seen—plastic cups and packing materials littering beaches so remote that no human had set foot on them, sea birds strangled in plastic soda can rings, sea turtles drowned in scraps of fishing net. Was there no end to the horrors?

Fighting a sob, she bit her lip so hard she tasted blood. Tears were oozing out of her eyes. *Don't! Must not let him see!*

She pretended to dry her face. The towel, warm from the sun, gave welcome refuge as she sank down onto the blanket.

It happened so naturally that afterwards she could not remember a point at which she could have rebuffed him. Rip's strong arm was around her shoulders, not possessively like Kevin's, but kindly, almost casually. It was the touch of an understanding friend. No words were needed or demanded. They just sat quietly as his hand gently stroked the sensitive flesh of her upper arm.

Gradually, Zephyr's posture softened. Gradually, almost imperceptibly, she felt herself leaning against the big, solid warmth of him. Damn, it felt good! Oh damn, why did it have to feel so good? So comfortable. So right. It was as if she'd been waiting all her life just to feel the comfort of his body next to hers.

But what about Kevin? What about the turtles?

In one quick move, she brushed off the towel and his arm and stood up. "I—I have to go now."

The look of hurt and surprise flashed in his eyes so briefly that she might have only imagined she saw it. When he stood up beside her, his face was set in neutral.

"Sure." He glanced at his watch. "I need to be getting back, too. I left Jackie alone with the shop all afternoon. If I don't get back pretty quick she'll slice me up for shark chum."

"I thought you were the boss."

"We take turns being captain but she owns half of the operation. If she got mad and pulled out her investment, I might as well scuttle the boat. I'd be sunk anyway."

Zeph bent over and picked up one end of the blanket. "She seems young to have that much money of her own."

Rip picked up the other end of the blanket. "Right on both counts. She's young and the money isn't exactly hers. She talked her father into using his influence at the local bank to get a loan. Unfortunately he's also pulled us out of debt a few times himself."

Together they began to shake the sand from the blanket.

"What does her father do?"

"He builds hotels. Or rather resorts. You know, condos, time shares, golf courses . . . The full package. He says he's going to give us the exclusive rights to a kiosk at the Wai Lana."

"He owns that? I've seen it on TV."

"Well, whatever you've seen, it's grander. And there's a rumor that he's planning an even bigger development somewhere here on Maui. Nobody knows where. If they did, you can bet the land price would go up. *Way* up."

As they talked, they folded the blanket corner to corner, end to end. With each fold they grew closer until he was standing directly in front of her. Bending slightly, he took the soft fabric from her lifted hands. And as he did so, his lips brushed, ever so lightly, ever so casually, the healing cut in the center of her forehead.

■ ■ ■

Rip whistled as he stepped into the shop's dim interior. The tune was left over from Christmas. What it was doing in his head now was a puzzle, but he didn't waste much thought on it. More interesting things to think about, like tomorrow evening and the date he had managed to talk Zeph into. Oh, he didn't *call* it a date of course. After all she was engaged . . . sort of. He had framed it as a chance to go over night dive procedures for next week, but it was a date. He knew it and he was pretty sure she did, too.

"Where the hell have you been all afternoon?" Jackie's voice came at him from behind a counter. Rip took off his sunglasses, then saw her clearly. Her dark eyebrows were scrunched into a furious frown.

He sighed. He'd been expecting this.

She leaned her palms on the counter so hard that he was afraid she'd break the glass. "I got your message but I was up this morning at oh-dark-thirty getting all the gear ready. Did we or did we not agree that on the days I did the prep work, *you* would be in charge of the shop in the afternoon?"

"Yeah. You're right. I'm sorry. Go home and get some sleep; I'll take over now." He tried to pat her shoulder but she jerked away.

"You're sorry? Ask me if I care. 'Sorry' counts for nothing in this business and you know it. Try telling some poor shmuck you're 'sorry' after he spends his vacation in the hyperbaric chamber in Honolulu."

"Jackie, listen--"

"No, *you* listen--"

A polite cough interrupted.

"Ummm, excuse me? How much is this regulator?"

Rip and Jackie whirled around and instantly put on their best professional smiles. It was as if Jackie had turned on a switch. Her voice was suddenly friendly. "That's two ninety-five this week. Normally they go for four hundred, but we're running a special..."

Rip breathed a deep sigh of relief as Jackie turned her attention to the customer, a tall, skinny kid with a shaved head.

Running the business with Jackie was getting old. Every time he so much as looked at another woman . . . well, darn it he'd never encouraged her. Never made her think they'd be more than business partners. So why this nagging guilt? He'd given her a chance to have a business of her own instead of some trumped up desk job with her father's corporation. He didn't owe her any more than that.

The buzzer on the doormat sounded as the customer walked out. Another one "just looking." Not buying. Ah, well, he thought. Goes with the territory.

Jackie turned back to him, her anger blunted by the necessity to be pleasant for a few minutes.

"Hey, I'm sorry. Didn't mean to be such a shrew. Must be PMS again."

"Forget it. Now go on home. I'll handle the afternoon and close up."

"Right." Jackie grabbed her backpack from under the counter and slung it over one shoulder. As she reached the door she turned. "Oh, by the way, Daddy called. He and Gina want us to have cocktails with them tomorrow night on the *Seaduction*."

"Gina? What happened to Trish?"

"Oh, well . . . you know . . . " Jackie looked vaguely uncomfortable.

The old goat. No wonder Jackie was hard to get along with sometimes. Must be tough to deal with the succession of "Daddy's friends" each younger than the one before . . . He took a deep breath.

"Sorry. I can't. Got other plans."

The door, which usually stood open, slammed as Jackie left.

■ ■ ■

Walking by the harbor the next evening, Rip made a delib-
erate effort to avoid looking at the mooring where he knew
the *Seaduction* would be tied, looming over all the other
boats. Karl would be sitting in his ergonomic deck chair,
stringy tan legs poking out of his shorts like toothpicks
stuck in a potato. In one hand would be a glass of scotch,
in the other, a fat cigar. Maybe it was his imagination, but
Rip thought he could smell that cigar right now, fouling
the freshness of the trade winds.

Never mind. He had better things to think about.

His sneakers thumped on the planks of the Old Hawaii
Inn. Once inside, the smell was all dust and history. He
blinked in the dimness of the lobby. At the front desk, a
young Polynesian woman, dark hair wrapped in a thick
knot on the back of her head, sat talking on the phone. He
waited until her conversation concluded. Unconsciously,
he rubbed the back of his neck. He wasn't used to wearing
shirts with collars.

"Can I help you, sir?"

"Yes, thanks. Could you ring Miss Meyers' room for
me?"

"Sure. Do you know the room number?"

"No."

"That's okay. I can look it up."

She gave him a big smile. He realized with some surprise that she was flirting with him. He got that a lot, but
it still surprised him. In his mind he was still the geeky kid
he'd been in junior high -- before his parents spent their
savings on his orthodontist and before he'd gotten some
meat on his too-tall frame.

Zeph appeared faster than he'd expected. In his experience, women were seldom ready when they said they'd be. But there she was, floating down the dark wooden staircase in a cloud of gauzy white cotton. Her skirt billowed in the breeze that drifted through the open front door. The white tank top clung to her shapely, rounded breasts. Her red-gold hair curled softly around her face.

Rip's breath caught in his throat. God, she was lovely!

"Hey," he said.

"Hey, yourself!" She grinned, then looked down at her strappy white sandals as if suddenly gripped by shyness.

"Are you hungry?" *Brilliant, MacKinsey. Great opening line!*

"Sort of. I forgot to eat lunch. I started walking along the shore and before I realized it, I'd gone miles. I just got back about an hour ago."

"Which direction?"

"Towards that big mountain, Hale . . . Haleak . . . "

"Haleakala."

"Whatever. How do you remember all those names? They all sound alike to me."

"Oh, you get used to them. They sound alike because the Hawaiian alphabet only has 12 letters. That means the same sounds get recycled a . . . Hey, look! That's a pretty nice sunset, even by Maui standards."

They had moved out onto the porch. The sun, an orange fireball, seemed balanced on the horizon at the end of a golden path across the water. Towering purple and pink clouds wore rims of gold. And looking down into Zephyr's eyes, Rip saw the golden glints reflected there.

He'd been alone too long. Perhaps, if he could think of a way to get her to stay on Maui, perhaps she could be something more to him than just another customer.

4

A soft evening breeze flowed in from the harbor caressing Zephyr's cheek and ruffling her hair. To get to the restaurant where they now sat, Rip had led her a block away from the Old Hawaii Inn and up a wooden staircase, one story above the street. There were no outside walls, just a white wooden railing waist high. In the fading daylight, candles and lighted torches flickered. From here she could look across Front Street and straight into the thick leaves of the "World's Biggest Banyan Tree." It filled the whole of the square, one city block. Its huge branches rested on aerial roots like an elderly man with canes.

"The old girl's seen a lot of history." Rip followed Zephyr's gaze in the tree's direction.

"How do you know it's a female?"

Rip gave a rueful laugh. "She's beautiful and provides a comforting shelter, but she's been there more than a hundred years and she's not going to move for anybody. That square is hers!"

His tone was jaunty but with just enough of a hint of bitterness to raise her curiosity.

"Is that what you think of women?"

"Let's just say that's how I've experienced women."

"Anyone in particular?"

"You mean besides my ex-wife?"

A deeply tanned blond with an apron over her scanty outfit appeared from behind him.

"What can I get you folks to drink?" she asked, nibbling the end of her pencil.

Rip gestured politely to Zephyr.

"Just soda water, please."

"And for you, sir?"

"I'll have a San Miguel."

"You got it!"

With a nod she was gone.

Zephyr considered using the interruption as an opportunity to change the subject. Still . . . she was intrigued. "Would you care to expand on that?"

"I don't know . . . " He avoided her eyes and stared out at the tree.

Zephyr stopped breathing for a moment as she watched his profile. Strong chin; straight nose, masculine but with the nostrils gracefully curved; generous, sensual mouth, laugh lines deeply etched at the corner. Would those lips feel soft, tender against hers? *No! Stop that!*

After a minute he continued. "Maybe I'm afraid if I expand on that, you'll think I'm a cad. You know, one of those guys who goes around talking about his ex like she's Snow White's stepmother?"

He looked straight into her eyes as though measuring her response.

Oh, if only he knew her response, she thought. "I promise not to think you're a cad."

No, *she* was the real cad and soon, when he received a copy of her article along with a summons from the Feds, he would know it. The thought tied her stomach in a tight knot.

They were silent a moment as their drinks arrived.

Rip lifted his beer bottle and touched her glass "Okay. To secrets exchanged which, I guess, makes them no longer secrets!"

Secrets. Oh, yes. What if she shared hers? Right now. Would he understand? Would he forgive her? Could she bear the look of betrayal in his eyes?

Rip took a deep breath. "Her name is Linda. We went together all through high school. When I enlisted in the Navy, she wrote me every day. When I decided to take the SEALS training she encouraged me. When I went off to Iraq she waited for me. I came home. We had a great wedding. Must have set her old man back several K, but he never blinked."

Rip tipped the bottle back and drank. He swallowed then continued.

"But, now that I think about it, why would he? There was plenty more where that came from. He's a partner in a hot shot L.A. law firm, specializes in corporate law, mergers, stuff like that."

Rip twisted his beer bottle on the coaster, then looked suddenly up at her from beneath thick, curly eyelashes. "In a word --bor-ring."

Zephyr laughed and nodded her agreement.

"So when he offered to pay my way through law school if I would join the firm, I said 'no, thanks,' and instantly I became the bad guy."

She smiled. "I have a hard time imagining you as the bad guy. Seems to me you're more the James Bond, swim-in-and-rescue-everybody type." *Except sea turtles, of course.*

He gazed back out at the tree and at the water just visible between the giant branches. His mouth twitched as if he were trying not to smile. That deep dimple flickered in his cheek.

"Yeah, well . . . maybe that's my problem. Linda's mom told her I was an "adrenaline junkie." Linda's mom is a psychologist and she uses psycho-jargon like a ninja warrior uses the nim chuks. Anyhow, when I explained my dream, which was to do pretty much what I'm doing now, Linda let me know in no uncertain terms that it was unacceptable."

"Really? Why?"

"Ahhh, the fact that you would ask that question shows that you, m'dear, have not been bitten by the Junior League Uppitty Lifestyle bug."

"And what exactly is an Uppitty Lifestyle?"

"Oh, you know, the BMW, the house with furniture you hate but that some designer decided you *must* have, the expensive parties supposedly for charity but mostly to provide an excuse to have your picture in the paper wearing something that cost more than I earn in a whole year. But mostly it means staying in your own exclusive community or travel that includes dragging fifteen suitcases from one fancy hotel to the next."

"Didn't you know what she wanted before you got married?"

"She didn't tell me what she really wanted. If she had been honest from the beginning…"

Honest. Oops!

"…and even after that…well… I think I just let myself hope I could change her. Pretty stupid, huh?"

"I don't know about stupid. I guess it's just human nature to see things the way we wish they would be instead of the way they really are." *Like wishing we were just two people on a date? Focus!* "Now what was it that you wanted to explain about night diving?" she asked.

But Zeph was only half listening as Rip launched into a discussion of compass navigation and disorientation. Part of her mind was busy reviewing the long talk she'd had with herself during her walk along the beach.

It was about that kiss on the forehead.

Oh, yes. It had been a kiss, no doubt about that. Sure, it was just a light kiss, merely a brushing of his lips on her skin. It was perfect for maintaining deniability if she'd screamed. But she didn't scream. She didn't even want to scream. What she'd wanted was for him to deepen that kiss. To move it down … across her eyes, across her cheek … down to her mouth, her lips, her tongue. Her lips that were suddenly hungry in a way they had never been hungry for Kevin's kisses.

So what was wrong? There was no future for her with Rip. That much, at least, was clear. How could there be when her whole reason for being here, for meeting him at all, was to cause him harm?

But if she could respond that way to another man she certainly had no business marrying Kevin.

And why did that realization cause her such terror? It would be awful having to hurt Kevin by breaking their engagement. But how much worse to marry him knowing, as she did now with certainty, that she did not love him.

But that wasn't the cause of the terror. No, it was more personal than that. It was the fear of being alone. The fear of having no one, of belonging nowhere. It was fear of a life as empty as the sea she'd watched every day from her father's sailboat.

Maybe that was the problem. In high school she'd been so uncomfortable around the other kids that she'd never had a boyfriend. Boys seemed to be attracted to her, but after a few uncomfortable attempts at conversation, they gave up. Maybe if she'd spent a normal adolescence dating and going to parties she would have known how to distinguish love and passion from a selfish desire for security, from a fear of being alone.

" . . . but like I was saying, fear is the biggest problem in a situation where visibility is limited." Rip seemed to realize that she was distracted and in response had switched to instructor mode. He sounded as if he'd given this same lecture hundreds of times. "It's not the fear of things they *can* see that gets most people. No. It's the fear of what they *can't* see. What might be lurking in the dark just ahead."

"Kind of like all of life, right?"

Rip nodded. He looked surprised and glad to have her attention again.   "Yeah. And the cure is pretty much the same. The opposite of fear is trust. Trust your equipment. Trust your own skills and instincts. Trust your buddy. And above all, *don't* panic."

Panic. Of course. That was it. Panic at the thought of marriage. Maybe it wasn't lack of love for Kevin . . .

"You two wanna see some menus?"   The waitress was back with cardboard menus printed to look like tapa cloth.

"Hungry?"   Rip looked at Zeph questioningly.

"Sure."   She smiled. Her shoulders relaxed. Maybe the attraction she felt for him wasn't dangerous. It wouldn't threaten the secure life she had planned with Kevin. It was just a panic reaction to commitment. Natural enough. And as for the turtle article . . . well . . . she'd be far away before he found out what she'd really been here for. Maybe he wouldn't even connect it with her. She could sign it with a *nom de plume*. He'd never know.

Comforted by those thoughts, she enjoyed dinner far more than she'd expected to. The Kalua pork was sweet and juicy with crispy bits of roasted crust. The Hawaiian sticky rice soaked up the sweet sauce and the meal was completed with a dish of mango ice cream topped by tender slices of papaya that slid smoothly across her tongue and glided down her throat.

As they ate, Rip kept her laughing with funny stories about some of the overconfident divers he'd met. Apparently Chuck Crowley was just one of a long list of vacationing mainlanders who talked better than they swam. There had been times of real danger to Rip, but he related the anecdotes modestly, making light of his own courage.

"So is your name really 'Rip'? Like Rip Van Winkle?" Zephyr asked as they descended the wooden stairway from the restaurant.

Rip looked embarrassed. He glanced around as if to reassure himself that the flocks of strolling tourists that crowded the sidewalk were deep in their own conversations.

"When I was in high school, working as a lifeguard in Huntington Beach, I pulled a couple of girls out of a rip current and . . ." His face reddened. ". . . all the guys started calling me 'Rip.' Naturally, the more I told them not to, the more they did it. Pretty soon it just got to be my name." Light from the tiki torches flickered over his face highlighting his regal cheek bones.

"Then what is your *real* name?"

He cleared his throat and whispered, "Alvin, like the chipmunk."

Zephyr stifled a giggle. "Well my name is pretty funny, too. Remember my dad was a sailor, so naturally he had a thing about various kinds of wind. Zephyr, is a gentle breeze."

"Then it fits you," he said, "refreshing and kind." He smiled down at her.

As they crossed the street, he glanced up at the sky through the branches of the banyan. "Say . . . how about going for a little walk? It'd be too bad to waste this great moonlight."

"Okay," she said.

The moonlight was indeed great. Zephyr saw that as soon as they turned a corner and left the lights of the main street behind. The sky glowed a deep indigo blue. A huge, nearly full moon played hide and seek with towering luminous clouds.

"I remember this is how it was at night on our sailboat," Zephyr said, half to herself. "It was one of the few times I was actually happy there."

It was then that she felt her small hand muffled in the grip of his warm, big one. She should pull away, but it felt so good, so comforting . . .

They walked on in silence under the rattling fronds of coconut trees until they came to an open space surrounded by a low chain link fence. Just then the moon popped out from behind a cloud and Zephyr could see quite plainly the rectangular shapes of headstones.

"That looks like a really old cemetery," she said.

"Uh huh. It's the pioneer cemetery. The old missionary families are buried here. A few of the whalers, too."

He lifted the latch on the metal gate and it swung open. Together they walked along the pebbly path between the graves. Bare plumeria trees held little knots of flowers on the ends of their branches like bouquet offerings.

"Does this bother you?" Rip asked gently.

"No. Not really. They've been dead a long time. I don't imagine we'll disturb them."

He laughed. "No. They've seen pretty much everything." He bent slightly and squinted at a rectangular stone decorated with a carved anchor. "I guess this is one of those whalers."

They both leaned closer, reading the inscription in the bright moonlight:

In memory of Oliver L. Livingston

Of the ship *Serena* of Portsmouth, England

Who died at this place

February 5, 1845   Aged 23

"I'll be 23 next month." Zeph whispered.

"Awfully young," Rip said.

Zephyr wondered if he meant the sailor or her. "He was a long way from home."

"Yep. And he never got back."

"That sounds so sad."

Rip looked down at her. "Funny, I'd have thought you'd say 'that's what he gets for murdering all those gentle denizens of the deep.'"

"I guess the thought did occur to me, but he probably couldn't help it. Maybe that's just what the men in his town did. Maybe his father insisted."

Rip stood up. "And *your* father – how did you feel about him dragging you off to wander around the ocean?"

Zeph gazed up at the sky for a moment before she answered. The constellation Orion gleamed overhead, but the Southern Cross was lost below the horizon. She remembered how brightly the stars had blazed when seen from the deck of the sailboat. She realized that she missed that -- missed the stars of the southern hemisphere . . . missed her father, in one of his good moods, telling her their names. Out there, in the middle of the Pacific, you knew the stars were made of fire. They weren't the painted dots they appeared to be from land.

"I felt excited about it –- at first—when I was little. But when you're becoming a teenager, the last people you want to be with all day -- every day -- are your parents."

He laughed, a deep rich sound. "No kidding. My parents were great, but even so, I couldn't wait to get out of the house."

They walked deeper into the graveyard among crumbling old stones.

Zeph shook a pebble out of the open toe of her sandal. "I used to dream that I was going to a real school, with parties and everything. Then I'd wake up and we'd be anchored in a cove off some unbelievably beautiful place. Only to me it didn't seem so beautiful. I felt like I'd been hijacked into someone else's dream "

"Which, in fact, you were."

Rip's voice sounded so sympathetic that tears suddenly burned in Zeph's eyes. What was the matter with her that she was talking like this to someone she hardly knew? It wasn't like her at all. But unlike most of the men she had known, Rip was easy to talk with. That realization alone was enough to trigger her old shyness.

They walked on without speaking. The only sound was the crunching of coral gravel beneath their feet and the rattle of palm fronds in the wind.

"That one has a poem written on it," she said, mostly to break the silence. She pointed at a stone embellished with what appeared to have been angels before time did its best to erase them.

As Rip bent down on one knee to read the inscription, moonlight cast the shadow of his eyelashes onto his cheeks and highlighted the aristocratic straightness of his nose. Squinting at the worn letters, he read:

"'When caught upon life's mournful wave,

By storms and gusts of danger riven,

We shall then find beyond the grave...'"

"And . . . ?" Zephyr asked. It was like a song cut off before the end. Unsettling.

Rip brushed at the pale dirt.

"And nothing. That's all there is. The last line must be buried . . . or worn off."

Zephyr scrunched down next to him, tucking her soft white skirt between her knees.

"You're right," she said. "It's gone. So is the name of whoever is buried here."

"'Riven'" he murmured. "What rhymes . . . ? Has to be 'Heaven' I guess. Probably a missionary."

"If there is a Heaven," Zephyr said softly, "I hope my mother is happy there." She stood up, knees shaking. Was it the unaccustomed crouching position or the nearness of Rip? He stood up and looked down at her. The moon popped out from behind a cloud and in the sudden brightness she could see him clearly. The green and white Hawaiian print shirt he was wearing brought out the unusual clarity of his eyes.

"Zephyr, I'm sorry! Your mother just died and here I am dragging you into a cemetery." He thumped himself on the forehead with the heel of his hand. "Mr. Sensitive!"

"No. It's okay. Anyway, you didn't drag me. I walked in here under my own power, remember?"

"I'm still sorry. It was stupid of me." He stood and grasped her bare arms in both of his big hands. "Hey, you're shaking. Are you cold again?"

"You do think I'm a wimp, don't you?"

She looked up at him. His face was in shadow now and all she could see, or remember later, was the shimmer of moonlight on the palm fronds behind him. He said nothing, but scooped her hair back from her face with one cupped hand, pressing her tightly against him with his other arm. In an instant she knew that this was what she wanted though it turned her carefully planned life upside down.   Her whole body filled with a rush of warm, glowing joy that spread down her arms all the way to her fingertips so that when his mouth pressed softly, then hungrily on hers, her lips parted, eagerly awaiting his tongue. And their tongues met, jousting lightly . . . exploring . . . then suddenly . . .

No! Panic rose into her throat, constricting, threatening to cut off her breath.

Pressing the palms of both of her hands against his ribs, she pushed herself away from him and felt the night breeze suddenly cold against the exposed flesh of her arms.

"I'm sorry." Rip said, his voice soft, barely above a whisper. His face was still cloaked in shadow. "I know. You're engaged."

"Yes." She was thankful for the easy excuse though in truth she hadn't been thinking of Kevin at all. It was her own fear of the unknown that pushed her away from Rip. The unknown with no mother to talk to.

And somehow she was back in his arms again, sobbing against the hardness of his chest.

"Shhh . . . Zephyr . . . it's okay. I didn't mean to . . . "

She struggled to get her breath as if she were underwater. Drowning in a nameless rush of emotion. She wanted to explain, to let him know that she'd wanted this to happen. But the sobs that seemed to have come out of nowhere, engulfed her.

What's happening to me?

She fought for control. This was the wrong time. The wrong person. But it wasn't his fault. She would tell him that, if she could only stop crying.

He was stroking her hair, pressing her face against the soft cotton of his shirt. Rocking her a little. "Shhh . . . Sweetie . . . I'm sorry . . . we'll just forget this ever happened—"

"No."

"'No' what?"

She managed a deep breath. "I don't want to."

"'Don't want to' what?" His voice sounded patient, gentle.

"I don't want to forget . . . this."

"So don't." He sounded relieved. "I don't plan to." He held her away slightly, looking into her face. "You know -- this isn't the reaction I usually get."

"'Usually?'"

He laughed and pressed her against him again. "Well, I don't mean I do this every day. As a matter of fact it's been a long time . . ." He tipped her chin up with one finger. "Hey, is that it? Am I that badly out of practice?"

"You've . . . got . . . to be kidding." She was laughing now too, through fading sobs.

He shrugged. "With the dive tours we usually send a customer satisfaction survey after a few days. Maybe you could add a few comments to yours."

Dive. Turtles. Uh-oh.

How could she have stopped thinking about her mission? But Rip took her hand so naturally that she barely noticed. They walked across the pebbly earth back toward the street. He held the gate open for her. "So tell me about this sailboat you lived on."

She stepped back into the world of the living and took a deep breath of air that was heavy with the smell of flowers. "It was beautiful – shiny teak, enormous sails. But it was also a lot of work - sanding, varnishing. I had to literally 'learn the ropes'-- which ones to pull, which ones to NOT pull, and why."

Zeph slowed her steps briefly as she remembered storms and the strength it took to manage the sails. In her mind, she could hear her father's voice. With a tiny sniff, she continued. "My dad said school was a waste of time, he'd teach me himself and I would learn from travel. So we left from Long Beach and sailed down the coast of Mexico . . ."

. . . where I saw the turtles dying...

" . . . then out to the South Pacific . . . Tonga, Fiji, places you've never heard of. Mom was scared, but Dad said always said 'trust me' so we did. He got us through storms. He never got us lost. But when Mom started to notice dark spots on her face, he said, "Trust me Joyce, it's nothing."

"Oh." Rip said. "I get the picture."

"Yes. Well…the boat was fun at first, then it got boring. I thought about school and friends a lot. When Mom and Dad started to fight there was no place for me to get away. I just kind of made a shell for myself out of books and daydreams."

He squeezed her hand. "Not your average adolescence."

"No, it wasn't."

"So where is your father now?"

Zeph shrugged. "I don't know. Last I heard he was still sailing. Just him and his cat, if the cat hasn't jumped ship by now. He didn't come to the funeral. But then I didn't ask him to, either."

"Does he know your mother died?"

"He might have known she was going to. When she was really bad and I needed help, I sent a message through the embassy in New Zealand. I don't know if he ever got it. I stopped trusting – even the U.S. Embassy."

"I can understand that, but you have to trust someone."

They continued to walk, in silence now, under thick leaves that blotted out the sky.

Zephyr knew she should take her hand out of his, but it felt so right, so natural, that she couldn't. "I suppose you have to get up early to take out another dive group."

He squinted at his sports watch. "I guess." Then he stopped suddenly and turned to her. "Hey -- why don't you come with us? We're going out to Molokini Crater and I can pretty much guarantee a beautiful dive."

"Well, I –"

"You do need the practice if you're not going to make me rescue you again on the night dive next week."

Night dive. Camera. I have to tell him the truth.

Zephyr stared down at the leaf shadowed sidewalk and started walking again without looking at him. "There's something I need to . . . to . . . "

"Do? Like buying plastic leis for your wedding reception? You know we frown on those around here, especially for weddings."

Oh, yes. And the wedding . . .

Rip stopped her again and turned her gently towards him, both hands on her shoulders. "Look . . . about what . . . what happened back there, I'm really sorry. I . . . well, it won't happen again. I promise."

Zephyr sighed. She was glad of the darkness provided by the heavy branches overhead. If Rip had seen her face, he probably would have noticed her disappointment at the words "won't happen again."

"It's okay." She patted his hard forearm as he dropped his hands from her shoulders. "And as for the wedding . . . well . . . I don't think there's going to be one. It was a good suggestion about the leis, though. If I ever do get married, I'll keep it in mind."

As she heard herself saying the words, Zephyr felt a chill of fear although the sweet-smelling night breeze was warm.

Surprisingly, the fear didn't last.

The next sensation was one of bounding lightness, like having had your foot caught in a tangle of netting, then being suddenly set free. She'd known the decision was already made, known it for weeks. The strain of hiding it from herself had been exhausting. But she couldn't pretend any longer, not now that she knew what real passion felt like. To get married wouldn't be fair to anyone, least of all Kevin.

She would have to tell him as soon as she got home.

"So the wedding is *off*?" Rip stood still. With one hand, he lifted her hair away from her face. It was too dark to see his expression, but she could hear the concern in his voice. "When did this happen?

"I'm not sure exactly." Zeph began walking. Faster, this time. "I guess the truth is that I didn't know what to do with my life after Mom died. Kevin was just . . . there."

"And now he isn't. So the spell is broken and from a distance the prince can be seen as the toad he always was."

"When you put it that way, it sounds dreadful. *I* sound dreadful."

"No," He caught her hand and squeezed it. "No. I didn't mean that at all. I was just . . . surprised."

Zeph laughed, a small unfunny sound. "Me too."

They had reached the main street again and found themselves surrounded by streams of brightly clad pedestrians. A large lady in a straw hat bumped into Zephyr and glared. It became impossible to walk side by side, so they dropped hands and Rip fell in behind her.

Zeph's mind was churning. What was Rip thinking? Was he scared now that once free she would make demands on him? Was he wishing he hadn't kissed her? Was he wondering if he'd been the cause of her soon-to-be-broken engagement?

Was he the cause?

And when would she tell him the true reason for her visit to Maui?

5

Zephyr was soaring over canyons of clear, blue water. Her fins moved effortlessly. She must have acquired gills like a fish because she had the feeling she could stay underwater forever. As she swam, unencumbered by equipment, the world of air seemed dull and far away. The water held no chill. On the contrary, it felt wonderfully warm. Or did the warmth come from the strong presence next to her? Who was that person?

She tried to turn her head to see the man's face, but an insistent ringing sound distracted her.

The dream rippled, faded away and disappeared leaving her in darkness with her hand groping for the house phone on the night stand.

Who knows I'm here? It must be Rip. Did I oversleep?

She dragged the phone across the sheet. "Rip," she mumbled into the receiver. "I'm so sorry. I'll be there as soon as I get dressed."

"Don't dress for me, babe. Why did you turn off your cell phone and who is Rip?"

In an instant she was wide awake and sitting up. It was Kevin.

"Kevin!" She tried to cover the discomfort in her voice, but she was still too sleepy to pretend. "How . . . how did you find me?"

"Well it wasn't from the lengthy and informative email you sent me, that's for darn sure. Who's Rip?"

"I'm sorry. I meant to write more. I didn't know how to tell you that I'm staying longer than we'd planned. I . . . I was afraid you'd be mad at me."

"Darn right I—"

"But, how did you know where I'm staying?"

"I got the phone number of *Ocean Observers Magazine* from your last issue. I called and somebody named Angie told me where you're staying. I figured, correctly it seems, that you'd tell them where you were even if you didn't pass on that bit of information to your very own fiancé."

"Kevin, I'm sorry. I've been busy and —"

"Busy, huh? I repeat, who is Rip?"

"He's the part owner of the dive shop I was sent to investigate. I . . . I'm supposed to go out with him . . . I mean go out on his boat . . . I thought I'd oversss . . . Say, why are you calling me in the middle of the night? Are you okay?" She felt a sudden cold pinch of guilt.

"No. No, I'm not okay. I'm lonely. I thought you'd be home today. So why aren't you?"

"It's a long story and I'm really sleepy." She squinted at her travel alarm's luminous dial. Four forty-five. "It's just after four thirty in the morning."

"Is it? Well it's almost eight here. Besides I couldn't sleep. When are you coming home?"

"Kevin, I don't know. We need to talk but I can't make sense at this hour. I'll call you later, okay?"

"How much later?"

"Ummm . . . tonight. When I get back from the dive trip. I gotta go now and get some sleep or I'll be too tired --"

"Yeah. Too tired. Wouldn't want you too tired." His voice had a nasty sarcastic edge that reminded her of her father. "Well, watch yourself. Remember the stuff I taught you. The ocean's a lot bigger than your mom's swimming pool."

"I've already observed that," she said dryly.

"Great. Keep up the good work and *call* me!"

The phone clicked and Zephyr found herself listening to a dial tone. She replaced the receiver in its cradle and pulled the diamond ring from her finger. It made a clunking sound as she dropped it into the nightstand drawer.

■ ■ ■

She must have fallen asleep again, but she heard the rain splattering in the courtyard even before the phone rang for a second time. She swallowed hard and took a deep breath.

"Hello?" She held her voice carefully in neutral.

"Hi." The reply came back to her ear, soft and deep. This time it was Rip. She sighed as her tense muscles relaxed.

"Did I wake you?"

"Umm, not really. I was just about to get up."

"Well, you needn't bother. I guess you can hear for yourself that it's raining again."

"Either that or somebody's taking an awfully long shower."

He laughed. "Actually, you could say somebody's taking a bath. If this rainy season doesn't stop pretty soon, our business is going down the drain."

"You had to cancel the dive trip?"

"Yeah. I've called the other divers. They're upset, of course. Like I can control the weather."

"You mean you can't? I was counting on you."

"Well now you know. I'm not the All Powerful Oz. Want to have breakfast anyway?"

She sat up, pushing the hair out of her eyes and glancing again at the clock. Five after six.

"Ummm . . . sure. Is any place open now?"

"Kawika's opens at seven. I'll swing by with an umbrella and we can walk over. Unless you want to go back to sleep, that is."

"I'm actually wide awake." No lie. The memory of the conversation with Kevin prodded her like a sharp stick.

"Okay, see you in the lobby at seven."

"I'll be the one in the plastic poncho."

He chuckled. "What color?"

"Golden Arches yellow. It was the only kind they had at the airport."

"Another Hawaiian fashion statement?"

"I'm afraid so." She glanced ruefully at the muu-muu still dangling from a hook on the bathroom door. Even in the early morning dimness, the flowers glowed fiercely. "If I'm not careful, Hawaiian styles might start looking normal to me."

"And once that happens you're doomed to stay here for-ever. They'll never let you off the plane on the Mainland."

He sounds pleased at the thought that I might stay!

Her throat squeezed. A complete brain freeze struck—just as it used to do in high school whenever a boy tried to strike up a conversation with her.

"Zephyr? You still there? Don't tell me you went back to sleep so fas--"

"No…I mean yes. I'm still here."

"Okay, good. I'll see you in a few minutes then."

As she hung up the phone and slipped out of bed, Zephyr felt strangely warm despite the clamminess of the unheated room.

■ ■ ■

He was waiting for her in the lobby when she descend-ed the stairs into the gloomy, gray, early morning light. Lounging against the front door jam, he was taller than she remembered. His yellow rain slicker was vivid against the dark green, wooden wall. With one hand, he was ab-sent mindedly twirling the handle of his closed umbrella. The dampness of the atmosphere had tightened the curl in his hair. Weak daylight cast shadows onto him and accen-tuated the planes of his face—the high, fine cheekbones, the strongly defined chin. A sudden thrust of heat shot through Zephyr's body. This beautiful man is waiting for *me*, she thought in the moment before she remembered Kevin and the turtles.

"Good morning," she said.

He gave her a small smile as he stepped away from the wall and offered his hand for her to take. To her surprise she accepted the hand without hesitation. She even experienced a ridiculous sense of loss when they ducked out from under the porch roof and he reclaimed his hand to open the umbrella.

His umbrella was small and more than a little tattered. Their height disparity meant that in order to keep them both dry, he had to bend down, put his arm around her, and press her shoulder into the curve beneath his arm.

The wind blew sharp pulses of rain into their faces as they sloshed across the street and into the partial sanctuary under the huge branches of the World's Biggest Banyan Tree.

The events of the previous night heightened and charged the atmosphere around them. Zephyr could think of nothing to say, a condition that was not unusual for her, but she guessed that it was unusual for Rip. Their silence, however, was not strained but felt companionable. As they shared the cozy shelter of the umbrella, the warmth of a budding friendship synchronized their splashing footsteps.

The wind intensified pushing them across another muddy street where they began to run, hand in hand like children. Rip paused in front of a low wooden building. It was silvery gray from years of attack by salt filled wind and rain. Breathless, they dashed up three sagging steps and clattered over the ramshackle porch. With one hand, Rip held the unpainted door open for her while with the other he shook his soggy umbrella and dropped it open under the dubious shelter of the porch roof. They stepped inside.

"Hey bro, howzit?" A huge Polynesian man, his hair pulled back in a long ponytail, was seated behind one of the round tables. The table, with its cover of red and white checked oilcloth, looked ridiculously small next to his enormous bulk. He struggled to rise.

"Hey, Kawika! Don't get up, bro. We can seat ourselves." With one hand in the center of her back, Rip guided Zeph lightly toward a table by the lace curtained window and pulled out a chair for her.

Rip ran his fingers through his thick, damp hair, scooping it back from his forehead. "Kawika, I want you to meet a friend of mine. This is Zephyr, one of my dive clients. Zeph, Kawika. He's one of the best cooks on Maui."

As they shrugged off their ponchos, Kawika heaved himself to his feet and slapped towards them on rubber flip-flops. "Aloha! Welcome!" He shook her hand with his huge one. With amazement, Zeph observed that his thumb was almost as big as her wrist.

Kawika grinned, showing jack-o-lantern teeth. "Rip always get the pretty ones," he said.

"Oh, c'mon." Rip plucked the menu card out of its holder and studied it. His ears flushed pink. "How long has it been since you've seen me with a new lady, let alone one as pretty as Zephyr, here?"

"Aww, just teasin' man." Kawika winked at Zephyr. "Seriously, it's good to see you wid somebody new."

Rip leaned towards her, pretending to whisper behind his menu. "Don't tell anybody, but Kawika doesn't think much of Jackie."

Kawika folded his arms and laid them on his massive stomach. "Better b'lieve it! She an' her ol' man, they de kine what's ruinin' this island with their big hotels an' snooty folk. They don' care. Why should they? Lossa money for dem; lossa trouble fo' us. Go an' fence off the bes' fishin' spots, bes' beaches. Where us locals gonna go?"

Rip tipped his chair back, balancing it on two legs. "To wash their dishes and change their sheets?" His sly smile indicated that he was teasing the older man. Zephyr felt pretty sure they'd had this same conversation many times before.

The tall Polynesian snorted. "Don' get me started again, Rip! It'll be lunch time b'fore you get any breakfuss, an' I bet this liddle lady here is hon-gree. Two coffees to start?"

"Sure, one at least." Rip looked questioningly at Zeph.

"She nodded. "Make that two, please."

Kawika's flip-flops clopped across the wooden floor and in a moment recorded Hawaiian music issued forth from the inner reaches of the kitchen along with the smell of fresh coffee.

Zephyr glanced around the little restaurant. The walls were hung with light brown woven matting. Green vines cascaded from baskets near the ceiling. The half-dozen tables that filled the room looked a bit wobbly, but cheerful with their bright red and white checked coverings and small candle lanterns. Through a door at the back she glimpsed a larger patio area heavily planted with palms and flowers which dripped noisily in the heavy rain.

"Well, I guess we know where Kawika stands on development issues, don't we?" Rip turned over his coffee cup and set it upright in the saucer.

"Somehow, I don't think his views are a surprise to you," Zeph observed, pushing up the damp sleeves of her green cotton blouse.

Rip gave a short laugh. "Hardly. Let's just say his views are shared by a good many folks around here."

"Don't they have a point?"

"Of course, but it's hopeless to fight progress."

Zephyr took a deep breath. "And what do you mean by 'progress?'"

Rip lifted one eyebrow, but Kawika's return with the coffeepot stopped his reply.

"Okay folks, what'll it be? Today's special's Hawaiian bread french toast with coconut syrup." He grinned widely revealing more empty tooth sockets.

After they had ordered and Kawika's flip-flops had clattered back to the kitchen, Zephyr was startled when something warm and furry brushed against her ankle. She lifted the edge of the tablecloth and saw a tiny black and white kitten stroking itself against her leg. As its eyes met hers, it opened its mouth in a pleading "meow."

"Oh, Rip, look!" She bent over and picked up the tiny creature. It was as light as a cotton puff. She laid it in her lap. It snuggled against her and began to suck on a button on the front of her blouse. "Where do you suppose its mother is?"

Rip eyed the kitten sympathetically and shook his head. "Who knows. Hawaii is full of abandoned cats. You can see them around parks and restaurants."

"How sad."

"Sadder yet for the native birds. Half the native species that were here when the missionaries arrived are now extinct."

Zeph looked at him sharply. "And you blame the homeless cats/"

"No, certainly not - not entirely. The rats and mosquitoes that stowed away on ships contributed, too. Humans bring change and change has casualties." He took a quick gulp of coffee and set the cup back on his saucer. "That's what I meant when I said it's hopeless to fight progress."

Zephyr stroked the little cat in her lap. She could just barely hear its purr over the sounds of clanging pots and pans in the kitchen. Maybe this conversation would provide the opening she needed to talk to Rip about the turtle riding. Maybe she could still help the turtles without hurting his dive business, but she needed a minute to think of the right words.

Fortunately, the return of Kawika with their orders gave her that time. She placed the kitten gently on the floor, drew a deep breath and proceeded. "Progress doesn't have to mean destroying the environment and the creatures that live in it. The world belongs to them, too."

Rip paused, his fork halfway to his mouth. He set the utensil down on his plate. "Somehow, I sense another stay-off-the-coral-type lecture coming on," he said slowly.

Zephyr pretended to be very busy sopping up coconut syrup with the chunk of French toast that was impaled on her fork, but she suspected that he knew it was just an excuse to avoid meeting his eyes. "Rip, I know that the turtle riding experience is a big draw with the customers, but it's harmful to the turtles. For one thing waking them suddenly like that . . . well, they could die."

Zephyr looked up quickly to see how he was taking her straight forward criticism. His face revealed nothing.

She plunged on. "I'm sure you know that they don't need much oxygen while they are sleeping, that's how they can stay underwater so long, but if they get scared, they could actually drown."

Rip's soft lips tightened ever so slightly. "You sound very expert. Where did you get your information?"

Zephyr's thoughts raced. If she told him about her work with Ocean Observers he would surely be on guard and then she would never get the evidence she needed. She would leave empty handed and he and Jackie would continue their abusive practices. On the other hand, she was no good at lying. Years alone with her parents had left her unprepared for the casual social lies most people seemed to generate naturally. She settled for a half-truth. "On... uh...the Internet"

Rip managed to smile without really looking amused. "And you believe everything you read on the internet."

"No!" She heard the harsh defensiveness in her voice and forced herself to remain calm and rational. "But you forget that I lived at sea for years. I know from experience lots of things about sea turtles. They like to be scratched on their shells. Their shells have feeling just like your skin does, so think how traumatic being ridden is for them."

Rip picked up his coffee cup and leaned back in his chair. He held the cup handle in his right hand and balanced it against the tented fingers of his left hand. He didn't speak for a long minute, his face betraying very little emotion. Zephyr felt a bit of French toast slip up from her stomach into her mouth. She swallowed quickly hoping that he didn't notice.

When Rip finally spoke it was in a low, calm voice. "Okay, let's say that the facts you've presented are true. Let's even say that I agree with you in principle – think for a minute about your own close association with sea turtles, hasn't that made you more aware of them? Hasn't that made you think of them as something more than just soup-in-a-shell?"

"Yes, but--"

"Just a minute. Let me finish before you answer." He leaned forward, setting the cup quietly in its saucer and looking straight into her eyes. "What I'm saying is that although some individual animals may be harmed by close association with humans, the dolphins in small tanks at sea life parks, for instance, the total effect on society has been an increased ecological awareness that benefits all members of the species. Do you think we would have 'dolphin safe tuna' without Flipper?"

"I don't know. We didn't have TV in the South Pacific."

"What I'm trying to tell you is that these issues are more complex than they seem." He leaned down and scooped up the kitten. Tilting his chair so far back on two legs that she worried for his balance, he set the small creature gently in his lap and began to pet it, all the time not taking his eyes off Zephyr. "Did you know that one of the proposals for safe guarding turtle hatchlings is that the animals that prey on them, animals that include, by the way, stray cats, be euthanized?"

Zephyr felt a flash of heat race up her cheeks. "So that's your answer? Save one animal by killing another? Do you realize that the life forms which have done more damage to the environment than any other ... are humans?"

"And what would you have us do? Euthanize half the human population of Hawaii? The needs of people have to be taken into account, too."

"Needs? Needs?" She felt her pulse pounding in her neck. "Do people *need* more luxury hotels? Do they *need* cheap thrills provided by unscrupulous dive services?"

"Now just hold on a second." Rip's voice was suddenly angry, his green eyes stone cold. "Trust me I can match my scruples against any--"

Zephyr stood up so quickly that her chair fell over with a crash, bringing Kawika to the kitchen door. "Trust you? Now where have I heard *that* before? You boat captains are all alike, aren't you. The Captain Bly Complex, 'that's the way it is because I say so and don't talk back!'"

Turning, she ran from the restaurant, out the door, across the porch and out into the rain without looking back at the shocked expressions she knew would be on the faces of the two men who had witnessed her outburst.

The sudden drenching of the rain brought her back to awareness of how she had overreacted. Embarrassment squelched her anger.

Now I've done it! Blown my chance of getting the pictures. Blown any chance of something between us.

She heard the sound of splashing feet behind her then felt Rip's strong hand on her shoulder. "Hey," he said in a low husky voice. "Hey. I'm sorry." Tenderly he turned her toward him and folded her into his arms. "I know your history with your father. I should have known how much that 'trust me' phrase would upset you. It just slipped out. Can you forgive me?"

She looked up at him, his hair dripping into his eyes, face gleaming with rain. He looked so earnest. How amazing to hear a man actually apologize!

"There's nothing to forgive. I'm sorry I behaved so stupidly." She raised one hand to try to brush the rain soaked hair off her face. "I . . . since my mother died I've been acting weird like that sometimes. I'm not usually like that."

He held her against him gently removing a strand of her hair from the corner of her mouth where it had stuck. "Of course you're going to be emotionally ragged for a while. It would be surprising if you weren't."

"But I thought I was prepared for her . . . I knew it was coming."

"I don't think we're ever prepared for the loss of a parent. My dad died last year. Heart attack."

"I'm so sorry," she said gently. Raindrops glided across her upturned face.

"Thanks. Now... how about we get you out of this rain before you start getting hypothermic again?" With his arm around her shoulders, he led her through the puddles and back to the shelter of the porch.

■ ■ ■

Rain dripped from the eaves of the old hotel all afternoon. It was still dripping as the yellow lights came on in the courtyard. A chilling dampness sent Zephyr to her suitcase for the heaviest sweater she'd brought along. She'd been sitting for hours nearly motionless in front of the LCD screen of her laptop. She had deleted whatever words appeared there almost as fast as she'd written them.

"As if fishing nets and plastic bags were not enough, the turtles of Maui are facing yet another threat…"

"No!" she hissed at the screen, pressing the delete button again.

"Several weeks ago our editorial staff received an email charging Mid-Pacific Diving Adventures, based in Lahaina, Maui, with…"

She pressed her forehead against the bumpy edge of the rattan table top. Her fingers hit "delete" one more time. She didn't even need to look at the keyboard anymore to find that button. Why couldn't she write this article? It was her big chance to get a more permanent job with Ocean Observers. More importantly, it was a story that needed to be told. So *what was her problem?*

With her eyes shut she could see the problem as clearly as if he were standing in front of her. Green eyes, dark lashes, the smile lines at the corners of his mouth . . His voice, deep and strong, yet at the same time kind and gentle. . . The easy, good-natured laugh . . .

From the dining room downstairs delicious smells of roasting pork and frying onions wafted into her room. Maybe food was what she needed. That must be the problem. She hadn't eaten since breakfast. Maybe she was too hungry to write.

Stiffly, she stood up. All of the exercise of the past few days had settled into a dull ache in her legs and shoulders. She rubbed her back. If only there were someone to talk this over with. If only Momma were here.

But there was no one. No one except Kevin, and he was the last person she wanted to talk with right now. She'd have to tell him, of course. As soon as she went back she'd have to tell him the wedding was off.

. . . and then what. . .?

Should she come back to Maui? If she finished the article she couldn't ever come back. How could she face Rip? And yet the thought of never seeing him again filled her with desolation. She wandered to the window and looked out into the courtyard where dripping leaves were turning gray in the twilight. What could she possibly do? Time was running out. Today was Wednesday. On Saturday there would be another night dive and she would have to decide if she was going to take the incriminating photos and lose any possibility of a relationship with Rip, or if she was going to forget the whole thing, lose her big chance at a meaningful job and, in the process, betray her commitment to environmental responsibility. She had to find an answer soon.

"Oh, help!" she breathed softly to no one.

There was no answer except for the patter of the rain.

6

The rain continued to fall all night so Zephyr wasn't surprised to hear the phone ring in the still-dark, early morning. This time she'd been half awake when she picked up the receiver. She spoke a cautious, "hello?" hoping that the voice she was about to hear wouldn't be Kevin's.

It wasn't. It was Rip's. "I guess I don't have to tell you that we got shut out again."

The sound of his voice flustered her so unexpectedly that she had to take a deep breath before she could speak. "No. I figured that out for myself. Sorry, though. I know the rain is bad for your business."

"Yeah, well… Jackie wanted to go out anyway, but after what happened to you the other night, I told her, 'no way.' If I had to call the paramedics twice in one week our insurance agent would have a stroke."

"Wouldn't want that."

"Nope. The poor guy will be retiring soon. Wouldn't want to spoil his plans to go to the Mainland and buy a Winnebago."

There was a small, awkward silence. He cleared his throat. "Tell you what, though . . . according to the marine weather forecast, this storm is supposed to be moving out by late afternoon. If it does, the sunset from Haleakala should be amazing."

"Hall-lay . . . what?"

"Haleakala, remember? The mountain you saw while you were walking on the beach?"

"Oh, *that* mountain. It looks like a long ways up there."

"Well, it's ten thousand feet tall, but the road is good. We can get up there in two hours."

"Really? That fast?"

"If we don't stop to look at the view. Of course that would kind of defeat the purpose of going up there, wouldn't it?"

Zephyr smiled. She shouldn't see him except for business. Being with him, feeling the magic of his touch, the comfort and delight of his friendship, was making her decision about the story too difficult. She shouldn't see him, but...

"I guess it would."

"Okay then. I'll pick you up at four if the rain stops."

"Well--"

"Oh, and wear warm clothes this time. There could even be snow up there."

"Snow? In Hawaii?"

"Ten thousand feet up. See you at four. I'll be doing my anti-rain dance."

"Me, too." She couldn't believe she'd said that. What was she thinking?"

■ ■ ■

The road was, indeed, good even though it was spotted with puddles. Water in ditches and fields reflected scudding clouds that alternated with the blinding brilliance of the late afternoon sun. Tree-dotted meadows wore carpets of intense, almost unearthly, green. To their right, the land fell away down a long, gentle slope into the vast and shimmering ocean.

"This is what we call 'Upcountry'." Rip had been glancing frequently at Zephyr since they turned off the main highway at Pukalani. She knew he was measuring her response and that he wanted to impress her with the beauty of his adopted home. There was a touching quality in his eagerness to share with her the sights he obviously loved.

"It's beautiful . . . and oh, look! Horses!" She pointed past him to a tranquil scene of brown horses grazing on moisture-beaded grass.

"Yep. People think we're all about beaches and fancy hotels. But this is the real Hawaii. This is the Hawaii that keeps calling you back."

"I can see that already." Zephyr continued to look out of his side window. She tried to concentrate on the scenery, but her eyes kept wandering to Rip's profile. His faded blue tee shirt contrasted nicely with the darkness of his wind tousled hair. Lines creasing the corners of his eyes could have been the result of many hours squinting into the sun, but combined with the smile lines at the corners of his mouth, they gave the impression of a man of enduring good humor.

Rip snapped on the radio. A woman with a very high voice was singing a Hawaiian song that would have sounded hopelessly sentimental anywhere else. Here it seemed exactly right.

"What does that sign mean, 'protea farm?'" Zephyr asked as the Wrangler continued to climb steeply. "What's a protea?"

"Those are funny looking flowers that people on the Mainland are crazy about. They are native to South Africa and somebody discovered that they would grow well here, too. Now it's a major crop."

"More non-native flora and fauna?" She looked at him sideways.

"Yeah, I get it. Like the cats." He smiled ruefully. "What can I say? Islands are fragile. We love them and we destroy them. I guess I don't like to think about it too much."

The same way you don't like to think about what you're doing to the turtles?

She turned her attention back to the scenery. The mountain rolled, smooth as a green carpet, thousands of feet to the sea. Above the water, towering clouds floated like sailing ships on the blue ocean, and the ocean, misty in the distance, appeared to go on forever.

As the Wrangler continued to climb, trees and meadows gave way to bare rock. The height was so dizzying that Zephyr couldn't look down anymore. But the anxiety brought on by mountain heights was nothing compared to the anxiety in her heart. She knew now. She was in love for the first time in her life.

But this meant that she had to tell him the truth about her mission. And this was the best time, while they were alone, to talk about the turtles.

Rip?"

"Yeah?" He smiled at her and put his hand on her knee.

She felt as if her heart were breaking. "I want to talk to you about the turtles."

He gave her a glance that was so sympathetic she couldn't force any words from her constricted throat.

"I know." His voice was kind.

"You...you *do*?"

"Sure. I knew you were pretty upset the other day when you saw the turtles with tumors. I can tell by the sound of your voice you're feeling sad."

Oh.

She had hoped that this was going to be easy. No such luck.

As he spoke, Rip kept his eyes on the road which was becoming increasingly steep. "Actual there are scientists at Duke University working on the problem. See, tumors appear mostly in areas where there has been a lot of so called 'development.' That's the reason Maui's turtle population has been so badly affected." He moved his hand away from her knee to keep both hands on the wheel. "One year ninety percent of the dead turtles found on Maui had at least some tumors."

"You mean it's fatal?"

"Eventually, yes. They go blind and starve."

Zephyr felt sick, her own problems forgotten. "What can we do?"

"Well, since we can't prove a cause, we don't have a cure. If I had a million bucks I'd start a center where scientists could come and study the disease. Trouble is, it's the developers who have the money. It's not in their interest to have people find out that they are the ones who are somehow causing this."

"No." Zephyr shook her head sadly. "I guess not."

Rip pulled off the road and parked. This time they seemed to be on the very top of the world looking down on roiling clouds.

"It's jacket time!" Rip grabbed his jean jacket from the back seat and also handed Zeph a pea coat. "It'll be way too big for you, but I didn't think you'd have brought anything warm enough." He winked in case she didn't catch the reference.

When she opened the door and stepped out onto a fine coating of snow, she realized he was right again. She couldn't have imagined it would be this cold in Hawaii. Buffeted by bitter wind, they slogged up the path that led the from the parking lot to the top of the mountain.

As they climbed, an awesome sight spread out before Zeph's astonished eyes. A crater, totally barren and jagged with smaller peaks, stretched for what appeared to be miles to the far rim. In the slanting light of sunset, black crevasses edged craters while monumental clouds rushed ahead of their shadows. Yet Zephyr's indrawn breath of amazement came not from the sights, but from the total lack of sound. The majestic silence contrasted eerily with the boiling, rushing movements of the clouds. "It's like the world must have been at the beginning of time." She whispered the words although they were alone on the viewing platform. The silence of the immense panorama was as commanding as the silence of a library. They drew close together for warmth, Rip wrapping her in the security of his arms while gradually a rainbow appeared, seemingly, from the center of the crater.

As they watched, sunset lit the sky with orange fire that faded finally into vivid blue, luminous with the light of the rising moon. It was only then that Zephyr realized her feet, clad in flimsy sandals, were freezing.

"We should probably be getting back," she said. She peered up at him from within the circle of his arms, trying not to notice how perfectly she fit into the center of him.

"I guess so. With the storm clearing, it looks like tomorrow will finally be the day for Molokini. We'll need to get an early start."

As they moved back towards the car, Rip sheltered her from the wind with his body. Still she was shivering by the time they reached the car.

He bundled her inside and turned on the heater. "Stick with me, kid, and eventually you'll freeze to death." Although his words were light, he looked concerned.

"Oh, Rip! It was worth it!"

He smiled, pleased that he had pleased her. "Pretty awesome, huh?"

She nodded and whispered a soft, "Yes. Thank you for this!"

■ ■ ■

When Rip stopped the Wrangler in front of the Old Hawaii Inn, the torches along the front porch were already flaring. A guitarist was playing in the bar. The sound of his voice floated on the trade winds. He was singing "The Hawaiian Wedding Song" in falsetto.

Zephyr opened the car door then turned to Rip. "Thanks for the gift of the sunset."

"My pleasure. We have one of those just about every evening around here. If you decide to stay awhile, I'll prove it."

Stay awhile . . . If only words didn't have to keep dragging her back to earth. She hadn't confessed her deception yet. So when would she? Would she ever? Shame heated her cheeks. She had to get away and think. But before she could slip out of the car, Rip leaned across the seat, held her chin between his thumb and forefinger, and kissed her -softly and deeply. Something she had never felt before stirred within her.

■ ■ ■

Rip drew a deep, satisfied breath. He loved the fresh, salty smell of the sea. He especially loved it in the newness and promise of a Hawaii morning. A misty squall hid the rounded outline of the island of Lanai, but the sky overhead was a perfect blue. The *Ipo Nui* bounded over the water like a joyful animal let out for a morning walk. Rip tried to banish all thought from his mind and concentrate only on the feel of wind and spray, but the presence of Jackie, standing next to him on the bridge, was impossible to ignore.

"What do you mean 'she's coming along as a free-bee?'" Her jaw muscles were twitching again. Always a bad sign.

"I meant just that." Rip expertly steadied the wheel, heading the boat into the swells. "She's my guest."

"Your guest?" Jackie flung her long, blond braid over her shoulder. "Now you're giving away dive trips without even asking me? Have you looked at our profit-loss statements lately?" She grabbed a quick sip of coffee from a mug decorated with their logo -a sea turtle. If you think I'm going to Daddy for another loan, you'd better think again. No way am I listening to another one of his lectures. Last time--"

"Hey, chill out." Rip reached out to pat her shoulder, but she twitched out of reach. Several drops of coffee flew onto her blue neoprene dive vest. "I keep telling you we'll be okay. The season doesn't even begin until next month."

"Oh, right! That's what you said *last* month!" Her mouth tightened into a grim line.

Rip squinted into the brilliance of the morning sun. "And if we hadn't had this long rainy spell--"

"If . . . if The road to bankruptcy is paved with' if s.' That was part of Daddy's lecture last time." Jackie snatched another quick swallow from her coffee cup before she slammed it into the cup holder on the instrument panel.

Rip took a deep breath. "Jackie. Look down there on the deck. How many divers do you see? You know we've got plenty of room. So what's your problem?"

He tried to sound calm and reasonable, but there was an edge to his voice that he couldn't quite control.

Control. Yeah, that was his problem lately. That was his problem since the girl with the golden eyes swam into his life. She was making him feel things he thought he'd given up on. After breaking it off with Linda and her Mercedes, he'd vowed never again--

"Rip! I'm talking to you! You could at least do me the courtesy of listening."

"Ummm... Sorry. What was that now?"

"I said . . . oh, never mind. You're going to damn well do as you please no matter what I say. You always do!"

Rip swallowed an irritated retort. What could he say? She was right. He would do as he pleased. And what pleased him most, suddenly, was Zephyr. Now with Kevin out of the picture, or at least fading into an out-of-focus blur, well . . . who knows?

Plowing into the indigo blue water, the *Ipo Nui* leapt from wave crest to wave crest throwing up streams of silvery spray from her bow. Rip's practiced eye caught a glint of deeper silver and a dark dorsal fin riding the bow wake. Soon the fin was joined by another and yet another. All around the bow of the boat, dolphins leapt and twirled in the air. Rip reached for the intercom mike and snapped it out of its cradle on the dash.

"Okay, folks, you're in for a treat today! If you make your way carefully to the bow, you'll see that we've been joined by some dolphins out for a good time. For some reason that nobody understands, they love to ride the bow wakes of boats. It's kinda like a kid on a skateboard hanging onto the back of a bus. A lot safer, though."

The passengers, Zephyr, dressed in jeans and her bikini top, and two husky firefighters from Cleveland, hurried along the gunwales and leaned over the bow railing. The firefighters whooped in delight, their voices drifting up to the bridge over the roar of the twin diesels.

"Hooooeeeee!"

The one with the shaggy moustache jabbed his buddy in the ribs with his elbow. "Now that's somethin' we'd never of seen in Lake Erie!"

"Yeah, Mike. I guess the nine hours on the plane was worth it after all."

"And you wanted to go to Vegas -Hey, look! Molokini dead ahead!"

Looming in front of them, still shadowed in the early morning sun, stood a strange, barren island the shape and color of a croissant. When they were just outside the curve of the crescent's arms, Rip cut the engines. The boat rocked gently on the smooth surface of the sea.

Without a word, Rip gestured to Jackie to take over the wheel. He swung down the ladder to the deck, ignoring half the steps.

"Okay folks, c'mon back here. Dive plan time."

The three divers reappeared around the sides of the cabin then took their places on benches on the aft deck. Next to the broad shouldered firefighters, Zephyr looked even more delicate and vulnerable than usual. Rip's mind blanked for an instant as the waiting divers gave him their rapt attention.

What was he about to say? Oh, yeah. Dive plan.

"Okay, obviously this is Molokini. What you see here is the tip of an ancient volcano with one side worn away. The caldera in the center . . . for you Midwesterners that's the place that the lava comes out . . . "

The firefighters grinned good naturedly.

" . . . the caldera is shallow, 30 to 100 feet, average about 60, but the fish are great. This is a marine life sanctuary so they're all pretty tame. They'll probably swim up to you expecting a handout and we've got some fish food sticks here if you want to give that a try." He held up a package of the green stuff that the Fish and Wildlife people wanted them to use.

"Question." Mike raised his hand in good military style.

"Yeah?"

"We've been hearing from some of the guys that have been here, about the back side of Molokini. Understand it's a wall dive. That a possibility for today?"

Rip glanced quickly at Zephyr. No way was he taking her on a wall dive yet. If she lost buoyancy control -well, it was 400 feet to the bottom. But she'd be dead of nitrogen narcosis long before she got to the bottom.

Still, if these guys went back to Cleveland disappointed, it made bad word of mouth for Mid-Pac. Couldn't have that.

"Okay. Sure. Tell you what." He glanced at Zeph. "We've got different levels of experience here so I'm going to let my partner -" He waved at Jackie who was on the bridge looking sullen. "I'm going to let my partner guide you on the wall dive after Zeph and I take a look around here. Feel free to have a swim or snorkel while you wait."

He turned again to Zephyr who was slipping the strap of her face mask over her head. He could see her fingers plainly between the tangled strands of her coppery hair. What he'd noticed at breakfast two days ago, and then again yesterday, was not just wishful thinking. Her engagement ring was still strikingly absent.

■ ■ ■

Zephyr was surprised how much less scary it was to take that giant step off the back of the boat in the daylight than it had been in the dark. Now the water was invitingly blue. The fact that Rip was in the water waiting for her gave her all the confidence she needed. She stuck one finned foot into empty air. The next second she was plunging down through the water. Her wetsuit filled with cold water, but this time she didn't care.

Together Rip and Zephyr swam to the anchor line where she clung gazing through her swim mask at the sandy bottom sixty feet below. All around, as far as she could see, stretched the ocean, clear and as limitless blue as the sky on a summer day. She felt as if she were looking down from the top of a tall building, or perhaps from inside the dome of a great cathedral, a cathedral filled with color and light.

Rip's hands were on the rope next to hers, his body comfortingly near. Their masks were close enough to touch. His eyes never left hers. Zephyr knew he was watching her for signs of panic, but panic was suddenly the furthest thing from her mind. This was the world she had only glimpsed while snorkeling from the sailboat, essentially an outside observer. The shallow dive at Olowalu had been only a taste. This was the real thing. Now the ocean was a world that included her, accepted her as another creature of the deep.

Shaping his thumb and forefinger into the "okay" sign, Rip pointed to the bottom, forming a question with his eyes. She returned the sign and nodded eagerly. Gently, he took one of her hands from the rope and held it in his then, leaving the rope behind, they soared hand in hand towards the bottom.

Like in a dream.

This was Peter Pan flying as she had always imagined it. For the first time since her mother's death, she felt a wild surge of joy, of freedom. Vast blue surrounded them. Golden sunbeams slanted downward illuminating the glinting bodies of brightly colored fish.

Rip pulled her onward, over coral knobs and rocky canyons until she lost all thoughts of the world above. She was a sea creature now, gliding past silvery jacks and fluttery wrasse. She was one with the butterfly fish and the stately Moorish idols. Supported by the water, her air tank was weightless. Except for the rubber mouthpiece gripped between her teeth, she lost all consciousness of the fact that she was breathing air, that she was completely dependent on the air supply she had with her.

It came as a surprise, therefore, when they alighted on the sandy bottom, and Rip inspected her air pressure gauge. Still plenty of air. Good. She wanted to stay here forever.

Rip searched inside the pocket of his inflatable vest and pulled out a cellophane tube of fish food. He opened it, handed it to her, and instantly they were surrounded by a cloud of fish of all sizes and shapes. Above, below, on every side they filled her vision. Their busy little bodies, their gleaming tails and fins flickered in the slanting beams of light. Eager mouths gulped at the clouds of food, and nibbled lightly on her fingers when the cellophane tube was empty.

Then, seemingly out of nowhere, a gray, torpedo-shaped body appeared. The fin on its back was unmistakable. Zephyr's heart seemed to stop. She'd seen those fins in the South Pacific. She'd seen the fish on her father's line torn in half with one bite from them. It was a shark. With a quick flick of its tail, the parrotfish that had been nibbling at her fingers fled.

Moving without conscious volition, Zephyr recoiled. Her tank slammed into the back of her head. She was somersaulting backwards, rolling out of control into a rock. A hot thrust of pain hit her as she landed on her knees on the coral. The shark's flat black eye glanced at her without interest before he flashed away.

Instantly, Rip was beside her. He took her hand and pulled her up. The pain grew hotter. She turned and saw the reason -- a crushed sea urchin. And she saw where its spines were. They were embedded in her knee. She recognized the disappearing shark as a white tipped reef shark -- harmless to humans. The big guy couldn't hurt her. The lowly sea urchin could.

It had. It sure had.

Rip saw the problem and shook his head sadly. He made a futile attempt to dislodge some of the spines protruding from her wetsuit. They didn't budge. Rip looked at her, shook his head, and pointed up with his thumb. Reluctantly, she nodded. Though the pain was searing, she hated to leave this magical world.

Hand in hand, they swam toward what Zeph assumed must be the anchor rope somewhere in the misty blue ahead. She had no way of knowing where the boat was.

Like Hansel and Gretel, she'd been enjoying the scenery so much that she'd paid no attention to landmarks. Now she had no options but to trust Rip's power over this enchanted world. He was her protector, Prince Charming in swim fins.

But she'd learned early that life was no fairy tale. There sure hadn't been any "happy ever after" for Momma. When Prince Charming kissed the girl it was supposed to make them sweethearts forever. But this was the Twenty-first Century and a kiss, even in an enchanted place like an old cemetery, probably meant nothing. She'd be a fool to think otherwise.

A school of yellow fish surrounded them for a moment like falling leaves in an aspen grove. The wonder and beauty of them, hundreds swimming in perfect synchronicity, almost made her forget her inner turmoil along with the pain in her knee.

Still, it was with great relief that she finally spotted the anchor line. From below, up on the dimpled surface, she could see the small, dark silhouette of the *!po Nui*. She squeezed Rip's hand in appreciation. He squeezed back, then placed her hand on the rough rope. Together they climbed slowly up to the world of air and everyday concerns.

Concerns . . . like her article for *Ocean Observers*. And Kevin.

Hands reached out as they approached the stern of the boat. Rip unbuckled the straps that held Zephyr's tank, then handed the heavy cylinder to the waiting firefighters. Freed from its weight, Zephyr lifted herself easily on to the swim step and sat to remove her fins, but when she bent her leg, she let out a yelp of pain. Rip popped quickly out of the water and helped her up on deck.

As gently as possible, he pulled off her wetsuit, unavoidably snapping the urchin spines as he did so. When Zephyr couldn't suppress a squeak of discomfort, she was positive she heard that tall, blond woman, snicker. As Rip guided her into the cabin, she tried to avoid seeing the amused faces of the firefighters.

"Never mind them." He murmured soothingly into her ear. "There are two kinds of divers, those who have run into urchin spines and those who will. But . . . " He sighed, helping her to sit on a bunk. "I must say, I've never seen it done so thoroughly.".

The cabin quivered as the engines roared to life. Soon they were bouncing from wave crest to wave crest over the rougher waters behind Molokini.

Rip wrapped a towel around Zephyr's shoulders and knelt in front of her, examining the wound. "Just a second," he said, rising, "I'll get the first aid kit and the vinegar."

"Vinegar?"

"You never heard of that? That's the standard treatment for urchin spines. I'm surprised you never ran into that fact in your sailing days."

"That's because I never ran into spines in my sailing days."

"Stick with me, kid. I'll see that you experience all the unsavory aspects of the deep." He winked and disappeared through a door into the further recesses of the boat. In a moment he was back with the vinegar. He knelt in front of her again. She winced as he dabbed the cold substance on her burning skin.

"I'm sorry. I'm trying not to hurt you."

"It's okay. Doesn't hurt that much." Her fingers clutched the rough blanket.

"Being the tough guy again, huh?"

"Well, give me credit for trying."

He smiled up at her, his eyelashes, still wet were sticking together in dark, spiky clumps. "I do," he whispered, "I really do."

The engines shuddered to a stop and the boat began to rock, side to side. The anchor chain rattled its way down. Then, one by one, she watched the spines being dissolved and extracted. Rip's hands were steady in spite of the motion of the vessel.

"Two words . . . " A cold, female voice issued from the doorway behind them. *"Paying customers.* Do you need a few more words? How about, I'm outta here? If you should need me, I'll be in the water, with those *paying* customers"

"Sorry," Rip murmured to Zeph.

"I don't think your partner likes me." Zephyr tried to speak lightly, but to her annoyance the words came out with a tremble she couldn't quite control.

He gave a short laugh. "Yeah . . . well . . . there's a lot Jackie doesn't like. Don't take it personally."

"I don't but . . . "

He sat back on his heels and looked up at her, concern lining his face. "Hey, it's all right. She'll forget about it by the time she gets out of the water."

"No . . . it's not just Jackie, it's . . . I'm just sort of . . . like you said yesterday 'emotionally ragged.' First Momma, then Kevin and . . ."

. . . the sea turtles . . .

"And me? He regarded her steadily. "I've really been messing with your head, haven't I?"

"No." She looked away. "Maybe, just a little bit."

"Only a bit? I must be losing my touch."

She laughed, cupping the masculine roughness of his cheek with her palm. Like a contented cat, he pressed his face against her hand, deepening her touch. He turned his face and softly kissed the inside of her wrist. He kissed his way up her arm. Quivering, she let her head drop back as he kissed the base of her throat. She heard herself let out a deep moan. This was passion. This was desire like she had never known before.

His lips reached her face. The tender softness of his tongue touched her earlobe and her closed eye lids, then dropped to her mouth where their tongues met with deep and thrilling joy.

Slowly he stood, lifting her with him, pressing her tenderly against him, swaying with the rolling of the waves. The neoprene scent from his wetsuit clung to his skin.

Like that night in the bunk . . .

Zephyr's bikini top began to slip upwards allowing her breasts a closer contact with Rip's bare chest. Her nipples, reacting to his soft, curly chest hair, brought a stirring within her like nothing that had ever happened with

Kevin. The damp swim suit which had been starting to chill her grew warmer as every nerve in her body seemed to spring to life and glow. Then suddenly, he broke the embrace and held her at arms length.

His broad chest was rising and falling with rapid breaths. He studied her face seriously as if wanting to ask something deeply important, but it was a minute before he could reclaim his voice to speak. "I'm not taking advantage of you, am I? Of my quasi-medical role here?" His eyes held a hint of humor, but with a serious question lurking behind them. His gaze locked onto hers and she noticed, for the first time, flecks of amber smoldering in the green depths of his eyes, those eyes that made her feel as if she had finally found home.

"How could you be? I wanted this too." she whispered.

"Ahh, you know . . . about your decisions . . . about Kevin. Maybe it's too soon."

She bit her lip and turned her face away. Now was the time to tell him the real reason for her turmoil. Now was the time to tell him what she had come to Maui to do.

He clasped her shoulders. "You're sorry already, aren't you." His husky voice gave his words no rising inflection of a question.

She turned back to him, ready to speak the words that would make him hate her, that would turn his gentle eyes to stone - a transformation like the one she'd seen two days ago at Kawika's.

But words wouldn't come. Mutely, she could only shake her head and whisper, "No."

7

Zephyr felt a chill and realized that the breeze from the open porthole was blowing over her back turning her wet swimming suit into a cold compress. She shivered.

"Hey," Rip smiled down at her. "You're cold again. I'm beginning to think it's my fate to be the instrument of you catching pneumonia. C'mon, we'll get you something warm to wear and I'll fix you a cup of hot tea. Bet you didn't know I could cook, did you?"

She shook her head.

"Well, I think I got the spines all out but you're not going to be real comfortable walking for a few hours.

With one arm around her shoulders, he opened a door in the back of the cabin and helped her through.

"Where are we going?"

"It's a surprise." He flicked on a light switch. She found herself standing in a small room whose walls curved inward to a point. A double bunk covered by a bright quilt and heaped pillows filled the "V" shaped end of the cabin. The walls were paneled with rich, dark wood, polished to a high sheen and lined with book-filled built-in shelves.

Rip flicked on another light illuminating a tiny, but tidy, miniature kitchen. He popped open a cupboard and took out a tea kettle and a box of herb tea. While the kettle began to boil, Rip crossed the room in a few steps and pulled two sweatshirts out of a small closet that was hidden in the paneling.

"Here," He handed her one of the faded blue sweat shirts bearing the words, "*U.S. Navy*," and a pair of matching sweatpants. "These'll be a bit big, but I think you'll be more comfortable in baggy clothes right now anyway. I don't think you'll want those jeans on. You can change in the head." He pulled the other sweatshirt on and ran his fingers through his hair. "Then we'll warm you up with Chef MacKinsey's famous hot tea."

After changing into the clown-size sweats, she returned to the kitchen-bed-dining room.

"Have a seat," he said, gesturing in the direction of a cozy armchair.

"Rip, this is lovely! Do you live here?" She lowered herself into the chair, carefully bending only her good knee and keeping the other leg straight.

"Yep," he said as he poured hot water into two mugs. "Home sweet home!"

So the business was everything to him: his home, his livelihood, his life. Now she knew what she had to do. She had to call Ocean Observers when she got back to her room and explain that she couldn't write the story. Of course she'd eventually tell Rip what she'd come here for when they knew each other well enough to laugh about it. But not yet. This wasn't the right time yet.

■ ■ ■

An hour later, with the divers back on board, Rip stared through the windshield of the *Ipo Nui* without really focusing on the on the inky blue water she was plowing through. A memory of the texture of Zephyr's skin still clung to the palms of his hands. He knew her life was back on the Mainland thousands of miles from him, but the thought of her leaving made him feel hollowed out like an empty sea shell. How could this have happened to him? He was the guy who usually waved a final "aloha" at the airport with far more relief than regret. Was it just her curious vulnerability or was it, perhaps, something more?

"Hel - low!" Jackie, now at the helm, was gripping the wheel as if it were a wild horse.

She looked at him so sharply that for an eerie moment he almost believed she was reading his thoughts.

"This is your captain speaking," she said to him in a mock official voice. "If you'll take a look out of the port side of the craft, you'll notice that the scenery has changed. I thought you might be wondering why we're not going straight back to Lahaina."

He hadn't, but now he was. Instead of the jagged ridge of the West Maui Mountains, they were moving towards the great looming shadow of Haleakala which guarded the almost uninhabited south side of the island.

"You're headed for the turtle cave. What gives?"

"I do." She grinned at him. "Just to make up for my little snit back there, I'm going to give you the information that half the people on this island would kill for. I'm going to show you where Daddy's new resort will be."

"Why would you do that?" He swiveled the first mate's chair around to face her directly.

"I told you. I'm trying to be a good partner, Partner." Her eyes were invisible behind her Blue Blockers. They reflected only the sea and a miniature picture of him. "Besides, he thinks it's time for you to know about it now. He told *me* months ago, but now he thinks you need to be in on the secret too - so we can all plan for the future. That's why he invited us out to the *Seaduction* - the night when you had your mysterious 'other plans.'"

"And the reason he wants me to have this information, for which thousands would sell their grandmothers to a glue factory, would be what?"

She turned fully toward him, even taking one hand from the wheel in an uncharacteristically casual pose. "Because he wants us to be part of it. He wants us to open a branch dive shop there because he finally feels like we've got some business sense. *Now* do you see why I've been stressing over our finances?"

"Not really. Seems to me we're doing just fine like we are. How do I know I want to deal with the kind of jerks that five star resorts attract?"

"Are you totally *nuts*? Jackie ripped her sunglasses off, turning the full fury of her gaze on him. "Don't you see what this could mean? We could buy another boat. No more of this Captain for a Day stuff. We could each have our own boat - *all* the time! Hell, we could even afford to hire a crew and get a day off once in a while! Now *there's* a concept! A day *off*!"

She replaced her sunglasses on her nose as if to further cement the barrier that had grown between them. Rip struggled to remind himself that they had once been friends.

"Jackie, I'm really sorry." He leaned forward and put one hand on her shoulder. It was hard and muscular. He couldn't help noticing the contrast with the remembered imprint of Zeph's softly firm body. "I didn't realize how tired you're getting. You do need more time off. We'll hire some help as soon as the season gets going. I guess I just thought you enjoyed it as much as--"

"As much as what? As much as you do? Gimme a break! Do you think I actually like having wet hair and fingernail fungus all the time? Well, do you?" She pounded the steering wheel for emphasis after the last two words.

"Umm, when you put it that way--"

"What other way is there?"

"Well, for starters you might have told me how you really felt. If you'd been more hon--"

"Okay! There it is!" Jackie slowed the engines and pointed to a gleaming crescent of beach rimmed with palm trees backed by thick forest and towering cliffs. Rip's heart sank as he saw that it was indeed, a beautiful spot. Too beautiful to be bulldozed into oblivion for one more glitzy resort.

"There's just one little problem." Jackie lowered her voice to keep it muffled by the sounds of the engines.

"Yes?" His voice took on a cautious note. "What is it?"

"You've got to promise not to breathe a word of it."

He gave a little snorting sound. "Tell me first, then I'll let you know."

She went right on as if she hadn't heard him. "Well, you remember how I had an idea about letting the folks have a turtle ride -- something to give us an edge, to make our dive service stand out from all the rest?"

"Uh huh." He spoke carefully sensing dangerous ground. "And do you remember I told you not to do it? Do you remember that I told you that it is illegal to even touch a turtle?"

So why didn't I tell Zephyr that the turtle riding wasn't my idea and that I told Jackie not to do it? Was it because I knew I should have been tougher with my partner? Or... was it because I couldn't admit to myself that I was relieved to be able to look the other way while Jackie was helping our bottom line?

He cringed inwardly at the thought. What a coward he'd been to keep lying to himself and hiding behind a woman!

The *Ipo Nui* cruised slowly past the deserted beach which sparkled in the afternoon light. For the moment, Rip pushed away his uncomfortable epiphany. Jackie was speaking and he knew she was saying something that he needed to hear, even if he didn't want to.

"And do *you* remember that I told you it didn't matter because they would go away soon anyhow?" She smiled smugly.

"Yes. At the time I wondered what you were talking about. They've been here practically forever."

"Well, if I had scared them away and they went some- where else, it would have been best for the turtles - best all around. That was the main reason I was messing with them. Too bad the dumb things didn't go."

"Best for the turtles? Why?"

"Because Daddy's project manager discovered months ago that they were using that beach for a nesting site."

"So?"

"So think about it . . . remember the Endangered Species Act? If the Feds find out they'll delay the project. Maybe even cancel it altogether."

"Are you saying that would be a bad thing?"

"Honestly Rip, I can't believe you! You are such an innocent. Of course it would be bad! The news about the planned resort would get out and the price of land on this end of the island would go through the roof. If the resort doesn't get built, then you and I won't have this once-in-a-lifetime chance to expand our business."

Rip's mouth went suddenly dry. It was hard to speak, but the words poured out anyway. "Don't you understand? It's a miracle! Those turtles swam thousands of miles to get back to the beach where they were born! How can you--"

"Because we don't need them anymore. Frankly that's a relief I won't have to touch their nasty, icky shells ever again. It's really too bad the stupid creatures didn't get scared away. Now Daddy's going to have to plow up the beach this weekend so nobody will find out about the eggs."

"Damn it Jackie!" Rip shot to his feet. Too late he saw the faces of Zeph and the firefighters turned up toward the bridge. They had heard. Face hot, he sat down again and, in a hissing whisper, he said, "there is no way I'm going to let that happen."

"Oh really. Just what do you think you can do about it?"

"Report him to the authorities the minute we pull up at the dock, that's what!"

Jackie laughed harshly. "Good luck. Today is Friday, remember? To stop the bulldozers you'll need a court order and there isn't a judge on the island that would start anything that complicated on a Friday afternoon. Why do you think they call this the 'hang loose' state?"

Rip raked his hair back with his fingers and noticed that his hand was shaking with barely controlled fury. What was he going to do to stop Karl? As much as he hated to admit it, Jackie was right. There wasn't time to stop him through the legal system. Probably why she'd waited until now to let him in on it, he thought bitterly. Some partner!.

"I'll think of something." His voice was cold and steady. "And as of now, I'm ending our partnership. "

He looked squarely into her Blue Blockers, speaking, unnervingly, to his own reflection.

Her jaw twitched again. "You *wish*. Where do you plan to get the money to buy me out?"

His stomach knotted up. He felt as if the boat were sinking under him. His boat! It was part of him like an arm or a leg. If he did follow through and end their partnership, the *Ipo Nui* would be as lost to him as if it had hit a reef and gone to the bottom of the ocean. Jackie would get the money from Karl, no problem. She would buy his half and he'd be back to scraping barnacles off other people's boat bottoms.

Well, there were some things that were just unacceptable, no matter the cost.

"I'm sure that your 'Daddy' will be only too happy to give you the money to buy my share." He heard his own voice as if it were coming from a long way off. "All you really needed me for was my diving experience in the SEALs. I've taught you enough now so you can handle the customers on your own."

He saw her swallow hard then clench her teeth. "Okay. Fine. I'll have Daddy's lawyers draw up the papers on Monday. And don't think you can change anything that's going to happen at the turtle beach. The bulldozers are already there."

The *Ipo Nui* shuddered briefly as she bumped against the dock. Gripping the bow line, Rip jumped easily onto the firm surface and secured the rope around a cleat. He nodded curtly in the direction of the bridge. As if in response, the engines coughed briefly then were silent.

Zephyr wobbled a little as her feet touched the unmoving dock. Funny how once you got used to the motion of a boat, the body rebelled at a return to solid land. A return to Earth. That was how she felt emotionally, too.

Why did Rip seemed suddenly so distant and preoccupied? And what about Jackie? Zeph could see her glowering from the bridge like an approaching storm, not even returning to the main deck for the customary, "Good-bye and thanks for going with us" speech.

Zephyr shook her head in confusion as she recalled the angry sound of Rip's voice issuing from the bridge on their return voyage. Over the roar of the diesels, she hadn't been able to make out the words but the anger was unmistakable. Could they have been fighting about her? Clearly, Jackie was angry about her free ride.

But exactly what was Rip's relationship with Jackie anyhow? Rip had said they were just partners, but "partners" was a word with several meanings. Had she assumed the least intimate meaning out of wishful thinking? She watched quietly as he shook hands with the firefighters, a mechanical smile briefly lighting his handsome features.

Leaving her gear bag behind her on the dock, she moved towards Rip who had re-boarded and was now yanking the empty air tanks out of their cradles.

"I'll get your sweats washed and bring them back tomorrow, okay?"

Damn. Why did her voice have to come out sounding so timid?

"Sure." He didn't look at her. His attention seemed totally devoted to the heavy work of lifting the tanks from the boat onto the dock. She longed to reach up and touch . . . kiss . . . that smile crease at the corner of his mouth. Only he wasn't smiling now and something in the set of his jaw let her know a touch might not be welcome.

"Or I could change here and . . . " She coughed to cover the annoying tight sound in her throat.

"Naw, don't bother." He continued to concentrate on adjusting the knobs of one of the tanks. "Those puncture wounds aren't going to feel so great in your tight jeans."

"Ummm . . . I'll see you later then?" She clinched her hand until her fingernails bit into her palm.

"Okay. Yeah." He straightened up and looked at her, his expression blank and unreadable. "I've got to do . . . some stuff. Just leave the sweats at the shop."

She nodded. Something seemed to clutch at her midsection. Rip's biceps swelled as he maneuvered another tank onto the dock. It landed with a dull thud. Zephyr turned and started back towards her bag. Rip seemed to have forgotten she was there.

"Oh . . . and Zephyr . . . "

Her spirits lifted sharply at the sound of her name. She pivoted on one foot. But he wasn't looking at her. He was looking past her into the distance and combing one hand through his damp hair. She tried not to remember how his hair had felt as she ran her own fingers through it, just a few hours before.

"Yes?" she answered and scolded herself -- *don't sound so eager!*

"Be sure and get some antibiotic cream. Urchin spines are nasty little buggers."

■ ■ ■

Those sea urchin wounds were stinging again as she limped up the worn wooden steps to the second floor of the Old Hawaii Inn. She stumbled and lurched against the railing. One of the pant legs had unrolled, tripping her. She folded it up again feeling clownishly clumsy. Even with the sleeves and pant legs rolled, Rip's clothes were far too big for her. She'd be glad to reach the safety of her room where she could set down her heavy equipment bag, run a hot bath, and give way finally to the tears of confusion and frustration that now burned behind her eyes. With a weak, relieved sigh, she dipped her key card into its slot, then pushed the door open with one lowered shoulder.

And there, stretched out on the bed wearing tan shorts and a garishly printed red and yellow Hawaiian shirt and a flower lei - was Kevin.

8

Kevin's face lit up in a wide grin. "Hey, Babe! Surprise!"

A soft gasp slipped past Zephyr's lips. "K . . . Kevin! When did you . . . how?"

Suddenly it was as if she'd been split into two people: one who was feeling a sickening sinking in the stomach, and another who is pointedly remarking on that feeling, saying, "There dummy! I told you all along you didn't really love this guy. Is the sick feeling when you see him proof enough for you?" But Kevin had been her future, her anchor. Now with Rip suddenly so cool and distant . . . was she ready to face life with no one? All alone?

Then it came to her in a lightening rush - she already was alone. She'd been alone for years with all the responsibility for her mother. The difference was that now she had the freedom to set her own course.

She found her voice. "How . . . how did you get in my room?"

Kevin sat up, the flower lei filling his lap with a bright cascade of yellow, red, and white. "The Hawaiian chick let me in. I explained to her that we are getting married and I wanted to surprise you. They really get off on romance around here."

He hurled himself off the bed dripping flower petals on the carpet and opening his arms to receive the embrace he was clearly expecting. "C'mere, babe!"

Zephyr's feet did not move. She closed the door quietly, then set her equipment bag down with a thump. "Kevin . . . I"

He gave her a beckoning "come here" signal with both hands. "C'mere! On the plane I got an idea. Why not get married right now, right here? We can have our wedding and our honeymoon trip all in one!"

She shook her head. "Kevin I . . . we . . . "

He dropped his arms. Under his pale brows, he squinted at her. "We what?"

She had to tell him. He would notice the absence of her ring in a moment anyhow. There was no way to avoid it.

"I can't marry you." She couldn't look at him. She was afraid she would weaken at the sight of his pain.

"You're kidding, right?"

"No...no...you see there's been--"

"You're not kidding?" His voice didn't sound hurt. It sounded angry.

Summoning up courage, she met his eyes. "There's been a...a..."

"Yeah? A what?" He was frowning now.

"There's been . . . a . . . " She heard her voice tighten and wobble as if shredded by the words she had to speak.

"Spit it out, dammit!"

"A . . . a . . . change--"

"There sure has. You didn't used to belong to the U.S. Navy!" He stared coldly at her chest.

Navy? Oh...the sweatshirt! She had forgotten about that. Heat rushed up her face to the top of her head where it did a prickly little dance.

Still standing awkwardly just inside the door, Zephyr thought she should move somewhere, but there was no place to go that wouldn't take her closer to Kevin. Turning sideways, she leaned her back against the door frame. She couldn't see him directly from that angle, but his reflection glowered at her from the mirror on the wall.

He started towards her, bare feet thumping on the floor. The old boards creaked under his weight, now multiplied by anger. "I came here to give you another chance. To give *us* another chance. The least you owe me is some kind of an explanation!" He held his breath and waited.

"You're right. I do owe you that." Her shoulders sank, dragging her whole frame with them, but she still did not look at him. She felt an overwhelming weariness. He had come all the way to Hawaii to see her but all she wanted was for him to leave so that she could have a hot bath. "I guess the only explanation is that I don't want to get married--"

"Don't want to get married or don't want to get married to *me*?" His tone was bitter. His voice hit her like a slap.

She was tired beyond patience. "It's not what you think. It's not that there is someone else, it's just that I don't . . . I don't love you and so it's not fair to either of us to--"

"And you just decided this."

"Yes."

"And you expect me to believe that there isn't anybody else when just a week ago we were planning our wedding."

She couldn't avoid seeing his face reflected in the mirror. His lips, which had once felt so hot against hers, were curled into an ugly sneer.

"I guess you'll just believe whatever you want." She sighed and started towards the bathroom.

His harsh, threatening voice stopped her. "So who's the lucky sailor? Is it that guy you expected to be calling you on the phone the other morning? Is it . . . what's his name . . . Rip? Is it him?"

"Kevin, I . . . I'm really sorry. I was going to tell you as soon as I got home--"

"Tell me what? That you've got somebody else?" He stomped toward her and stood in front of her, blocking her way towards the bathroom. "Don't you think I figured that out for myself when you didn't come home when you promised?"

Her shoulders tensed ready to push him out of the way if he came any closer. "I told you, Kevin, it's not what you think!"

"No? No? Then whose shirt is that? And don't try to tell me you got it from a second hand store!" He reached out and pulled on her sleeve which unrolled and stretched out twice as far as her arm. "It's about ten sizes too big for you!" He gave the sleeve a sharp flip and let go of it.

Zephyr pushed the sleeve back up, freeing her hand from the long, cotton tunnel. "I wasn't going to tell you that. I was going to tell you that it doesn't matter whose shirt I'm wearing. All that matters is the ring that I'm *not* wearing. And I'm sorry, truly I am!"

She ducked quickly around him and, in two big steps she was at the dresser, pulling the ring out of the corner of the top drawer where she had hidden it under a pile of lacy underwear. Kevin's reflection loomed in the mirror. Kevin himself, face contorted in fury, stood close behind her. She felt closed in, unable to catch her breath. She turned to face him. Grasping his hand, she gently opened his clenched fist and laid the ring in his upturned palm. He stuffed it in the pocket of his shorts without looking at it.

"So where is he? Where is this turtle jockey?" His voice was hard, his breathing sharp and quick.

"It doesn't matter." Her throat was so tight that she had to force the words out. To think that she had almost married this man! How could she have been so blind? "It's not about him. It's about us . . . me, actually."

Kevin pulled off the lei and flung it to the floor. "We were just fine until you ran off to play with your turtles. Now, where do I find this guy?"

With a sudden sharp gesture, he raised his hand to her face. She flinched, but he didn't hit her. Instead, he was reaching for the back of her neck where the collar of the sweatshirt lay against it. With one swift move he spun her around and turned the ribbed neck opening inside out. He flipped a tag up and read it.

"Ha! 'MacKinsey,' Not a Hawaiian name. Shouldn't be too hard to find in the phone book!"

Zephyr felt the blood drain out of her face and sink into her furiously beating heart. "Go ahead if you want to make a fool of yourself," she hissed, shocked at the strength of her own anger.

"Or maybe I should just start asking around at the dive shops?" He frowned meaningfully at her equipment bag.

"Do whatever you want. It won't change anything." She tried to sound indifferent, but her heart was beating so hard that she feared he could hear it in the silence of the room."

For a long moment, neither of them moved. The only sound was the petulant squawking of the mynah birds in the courtyard.

"'Whatever I want,'" he mocked in a shrill parody of her voice. "What I want is what you just finished telling me I can't have." He plopped down on the end of the bed, kicking his feet violently into his tan deck shoes.

"MacKinsey." He stood and started towards the door. "Well, Rip MacKinsey, we'll see who's out of his depth around here!"

He jerked the door open, strode through it, and slammed it behind him without looking back.

■ ■ ■

Rip glared impatiently at his watch as if it were responsible for the fact that he's been on hold for twelve minutes and thirty-three seconds. His neck was aching from clenching the phone against his shoulder, but he needed both hands free to flatten the large scale chart of the turtle cave area. He wrestled it against the slippery glass of the dive shop counter top. It obviously just wanted to curl up and go back into the dusty drawer from which he'd yanked it the minute he'd returned from the boat.

Why now? Of all the times for Jackie to pull this . . . Right now he wanted to be thinking about Zephyr and how great she'd felt in his arms . . . as if they'd been made for each other. What he didn't want to be thinking about was how to stop Karl and his money-hungry crew. But knowledge made protecting the nesting grounds his responsibility now. No way to weasel out.

He hadn't looked at this map in months. He hadn't needed to. He knew the area better than the back of his hand. So what was he looking for? He didn't exactly know, but he was sure he'd recognize it when he found it.

Rip was studying the chart so intently that he didn't know how long the guy had been standing in the doorway. A crawly feeling made him look up. He got a quick impression of cold blue eyes under a fringe of pale blond hair. The kid looked angry about something.

"Yes? Can I help you?" He shifted his right hand from the chart to pull the phone away from his mouth. The map recoiled irritatingly against his left wrist.

"Yeah. You sure can. You can . . . " His teeth flashed white behind his tight lips as he made a rude suggestion.

"Excuse me?" Rip punched the disconnect button and set the phone down, giving the guy his full attention.

"You heard me."

Instantly, Rip felt something stir within him. Something like a fanged animal, every nerve on alert. It was a feeling he hadn't experienced in years, not since he left Iraq. He hated the feeling. He hated the punk for un-chaining it.

Forcing his voice to remain calm and steady, he held the kid in his gaze. "Is there something in particular you think I've done to you, or do you greet everyone this way?"

"Don't pretend you don't know what I'm talking about. You must have known she was engaged."

"*She?*"

For a split second his mind rummaged around. She? Zephyr. So this was Kevin. He willed his face not to betray his realization. Don't give anything away. Name, rank, se-rial number. That's all.

"Sorry, pal." He flashed a patronizing grin. "'Fraid I don't know what the heck you're talking about." With a barely perceptible gesture, he flexed the arm that held the chart. "Now would you please take your attitude and get out of my shop before I have to throw you out?"

"Oh, tough guy, huh?" Kevin did a preening shoulder shake. "Well, dive master this -- that cute little number you've been going down with is really an environmental spy. She works for Ocean Observers and she's here to write an article about you and your turtle riding gig. Besides that, she's planning to rat you out to the Feds." Kevin flipped his hair back from his forehead with one hand. A sneer crawled across his face. "So you can kiss your big shot dive business good-bye."

Rip set the chart carefully on the counter, buying time to process the information. His teeth were gritted so tight-ly that his jaw ached but he kept his voice level and his expression neutral. "We're out of the turtle riding business as of today, so your news flash is a bit late. Now, if that's all you're here for--"

"What I'm here for is to tell you that if you think you've struck it rich by netting yourself an heiress, you can think again. She's my little pot of gold and I'm getting her back."

Heiress?

Rip felt the blood rush to his face. His mouth went dry and his forehead oozed sweat. He'd never thought to ask her about her financial situation. He assumed her dad had spent all his inheritance on sailing. Now, just as he was beginning to think he'd finally found his soul mate … but another rich girl? Another girl who thought her money inevitably gave her the power to control others? No damn way!

Kevin's pale eyes narrowed. "Now don't try to tell me you didn't know about her grandfather. The old guy invented some kind of widget that goes in a cell phone. When Zephyr's mom got sick, her old man got an attack of the guiltsies and signed over most of the stock to her. Cell phone business went nuts, stock went through the roof. Mom died and now the whole portfolio is Zeph's and, until you butted in, it was going to be mine, too. I don't know about Hawaii, but Arizona is a community property state. You know *community property?*" A crooked smile creased his thin face.

"Listen, Kevin--" Rip leaned over the counter and using both hands grabbed the guy by the lapels of his garish shirt.

Kevin's eyes opened wide in silent surprise.

"Yeah, I know who you are, you incompetent jerk! I can get your dive instructor's certificate lifted with one

phone call telling P.A.D.I. about how you certified a diver
who never even got her fins in a lake, much less the ocean!
So don't you come in here and threaten me! Now take your
sorry smirk outta here before I kick it and you all the way
back to the Mainland!"

Rip forced his hands to open even though they wanted
to wring the kid's neck. Kevin staggered backwards. For
one long minute the two men stared at each other, then
Kevin laughed, a harsh unfunny sound.

"Well good luck, sucker!" He pivoted on one foot and
started for the door then turned back and, in a shaky voice,
added, "you're gonna need it."

The doormat buzzed and he was gone.

■ ■ ■

For a few minutes, Zephyr sat unmoving on the edge of the
bed. The extra fabric of the oversized sweats clung to her
skin, sinking her down into a pile of stifling cotton. She had
not even thought to change. From the bar downstairs she
could already hear the evening sounds of Karaoke.

Once again she asked herself bitterly how she could
have been so stupid as to even consider marrying Kevin.
How had she been so blind as to fail to notice his self-
ishness and immaturity? And now that she realized she
hadn't really known him, the thought ran through her like
an electric shock that she also didn't know what he might
do if he found Rip.

She sprang from the bed as if bitten. As she rushed to
get her clothes, her sandal skidded on the wilting corpse
of Kevin's discarded lei. Grabbing the bedpost for balance,

she regained her footing then gave the sad pile of petals a violent kick.

Zephyr stripped off the sweat shirt that had silently betrayed both her and Rip, then plopped onto the bed to struggle out of the over-long pants. Leaving the discarded garments puddled on the floor, she snatched a drawer out of the bureau and dumped it upside down onto the bed. The first article of clothing her shuffling hands caught hold of was a bright blue sundress with a scoop neck and full skirt. She popped it over her head ignoring her lack of underwear.

Once clad in her own clothes and able to move more easily, she dashed out of her room and down the wooden steps to the lobby. The large room was full of Asian tourists. She slalomed through the group. Her hip grazed a table holding a huge floral display and causing it to wobble. Bursting outdoors she began to run, darting through crowds of strolling vacationers, unmindful of curious faces turned in her direction, not seeing the colors of the sunset filling the sky.

Two blocks, three blocks… she scanned the fronts of the buildings: Tee shirt shop, ice cream stand, ABC Store… she'd only been to Rip's dive shop twice, once to sign up and again to prepare for the ill-fated night dive. Would she remember where it was? She had been focused on her mission then and hadn't paid attention. But now she started to run. She ran up the main street, then down side streets. It was growing dark. Nothing looked familiar.

But … Yes! There it suddenly was! She remembered the gorgeous poster in the window -- colorful fish swimming against a background of impossibly vivid blue. Gasping, she tried the door. It was locked. She shook the knob. She banged on the glass. Finally, she called out, "Rip! Are you there? Rip?"

In the dimness of the store's interior, she saw a large shape moving towards her. As the shape drew nearer, she saw it was Rip. Her shoulders collapsed in relief. At least he was okay. If Kevin had found him, he was undoubtedly furious with her, but he seemed to be okay. Kevin hadn't harmed him . . . at least not physically.

The door opened. In the dusky light she couldn't read the expression on his face but his body appeared unyielding.

"Did Kevin--" she began then stopped to catch her breath.

Rip did not move.

"Did he tell you about me? About Ocean Observers?"

"Yes." The harsh sting of his voice made her wince.

"I meant to tell you myself . . . I was *going* to tell you . . . "

Her voice trailed off. Rip continued to stand in the doorway, silent and still.

Zephyr waited for a moment, hoping he would say something. When he didn't she continued, speaking fast to fill the silence. "I started to tell you the other morning, at breakfast, but we got in that argument about the kitten . . . Then again when we were driving up the mountain I was going to tell you, but . . . And besides, I wasn't going to write about you anyway . . . I mean I *was* but then I changed my mind . . . "

If only he would say something . . . anything . . . anything at all . . .

She sighed and looked down at her feet. In her hurry she had put on sandals that didn't match. "I . . . I know how you must be feeling . . . how you must--"

"Do you? And just how do you know so much about me when, it seems, I know nothing real about you?" His voice was calm, quiet, but with an undertone of fury that chilled her to the bone.

"But you *do*, you . . . you know everything important that --" She became aware of an elderly couple standing on the sidewalk staring at them. "everything that . . . Can I come in, please?"

Silently he stepped aside and opened the door wider.

The interior of the shop was faintly lit by ambient light from the moon and the street outside. Zephyr still could not make out Rip's expression, his face remained in shadow, but he seemed to loom over her. His broad shoulders and wide chest which had been so comforting during their dives together, now implied a menace that made her shudder.

"So what is it that you want from me?" There was no water on earth colder than his voice. The sound of it filled her with a bleak emptiness.

"I . . . I guess I hope you'll understand." She expected some kind of sarcastic response, but hearing nothing except the sound of his breathing, she rushed on. "It's true I did come here to get incriminating evidence for Ocean Observers and I would have except that I lost my camera, you remember . . . remember that night?"

"Yes."

And, of course he remembers the kindness and concern he wasted on me . . . which he knows now, I didn't deserve.

"But then, after I got to know you I changed my mind but I didn't know how to tell you . . . but I was going to . . . and . . . and I wouldn't have written the article without warning you . . . " Her words tumbled over each other like people being pushed through an exit gate during a fire. She struggled for control. "In fact I wouldn't have written it at all. I know you have no reason to believe me or to tr . . . trus--"

"Trust you?" His voice fairly dripped with irony.

Zephyr's hands, which had been fluttering in front of her as if to pump out her words, dropped to her sides. "Yes, she whispered. I guess that's what I'm asking. Trust and a second chance."

In the dim light she felt, rather than saw, his bitter smile. "Didn't Kevin, as a 'qualified' scuba instructor and concerned would-be husband, inform you that in diving there are no 'second chances?'"

Now she was feeling worse sea sickness than she had ever felt in a boat. Her stomach seemed to be crushing itself into a tight fist inside of her. In place of words, the harsh taste of acid filled her mouth, yet there was one last thing she needed to say. She drew a deep breath. "At least believe this . . . " She swallowed hard. Even to her own ears, her voice sounded odd - hoarse and strained. "Please believe that I'm . . . I'm very sorry."

Gathering her remaining shreds of dignity, she turned, pushed open the door and stepped out into the crowded, lonely street.

9

He wanted to run after her. He wanted to grab her by the shoulders, give her a good shake, then hold her tightly against him and pretend he'd never seen Kevin. Never heard Kevin. Never heard those awful words . . . *Spy* . . . *Heiress* . . .

But he *had* heard them and now it was too late, too late to believe in the foolish dream of finding his soul mate - of finding real love. It was too late to feel her soft, yielding body against him. Yielding. Had that been part of it too? Was she deliberately seducing him? Making a fool of him just to get the information she needed, to get evidence to destroy him and all he'd worked for?

Damn. Of course! Only an idiot would think otherwise!

His mind began to run a fast replay of all those memories of the past week. Each scene had to be painfully revised now, in the harsh light of this new knowledge. Each tarnished memory brought a fresh sense of loss, a fresh and scalding grief.

He leaned his forehead against the closed door of his shop, banging it two more times, hard enough to hurt, hard enough to knock some sense into him. He'd been stupid to trust a woman again. Now Zephyr was gone. After this afternoon, his business was gone. Soon his boat would be gone. Blindly, he moved through the darkened shop. He knew it well enough to find his way without light anywhere he wanted to go . . . as soon as he figured out where he wanted to go.

Then his foot kicked something unexpected. Something light yet large and crinkly. Acting on unthinking reflex, he bent over and picked it up. It was the chart he'd been studying when Kevin walked into the shop, and into his life. Must have been sucked off the counter by a gust of air as Kevin slammed the door on his way out. Rip leaned against the cold glass counter top, rolling and unrolling the map a few times just because his hands needed something to do.

Wait a second!

Something like a voice was telling him he had nothing left to lose and that was a kind of freedom. He could do something radical. He could do that which he had been warily considering when Kevin barged in and changed his life.

Quickly, he reached for the light switch and snapped it on. The room sprang into brightness. He laid the chart out flat on the counter. He couldn't save his business or his dreams, but at least he could save the turtle nesting site.

Now he knew what he'd been looking for, why he was studying the chart when Kevin had interrupted him. The turtle cave. How could he have not remembered that it wasn't just a cave, but a tunnel? It was a tunnel to the beach and a perfect spot from which to sabotage Karl's greedy plans. Okay, so it wouldn't stop development forever, but at least he could temporarily disable the bulldozers. He could stall them until he could get in touch with someone official next week.

He poured the energy from his anger and disappointment into action, glancing around the store and mentally listing all the equipment he would need. A few tools, wouldn't take much, just a well-placed wrench or two and the sand that was already there. He'd need extra air to get through the tunnel and out again . . . and . . . coffee. Lots of coffee. He would be up all night and he needed to stay alert.

First rule of diving - never dive alone.

But he would be alone and his mission, his very life depended on his ability to keep his focus.

He glanced at the dive watch on his wrist. Eight fifteen. He remembered he hadn't eaten since breakfast, but he would need all his strength. Kawika would still be cooking. Ought to grab a quick bite and a thermos of coffee. Better to wait until later anyway, when the security guards would be getting sleepy. The beach would be well-guarded, of that he was sure. Tucking the chart under his arm, he snapped off the light and let himself out, locking the door behind him.

■ ■ ■

The tiny restaurant was empty except for a young couple finishing their dinner at a corner table. Honeymooners. The total attention they fixed on each other would have given them away even if their sparkling new rings and slightly wilted leis hadn't. Rip felt a terrible pang of loss as he remembered Zephyr sitting at that very same table in the corner, bright hair beaded with raindrops, golden eyes clear and without guile.

Without guile. Ha! That was a good one.

He forced his thoughts back to his mission. He could think about Zephyr later. Later and for the rest of his life.

"Hey, Bro! Howzit?"

Rip jumped slightly at the voice behind him. His nerves were tight like a cat on a birding expedition. "Hey, Kawika. What are you cooking tonight?"

"Spam an' eggs. Official state food of Hawaii."

Rip pulled out a chair and seated himself on one side of a table set for two. "Okay. I'll have that and coffee." Without conscious awareness, he lapsed into the Pidgin dialect. "Plenty coffee."

"C'min' right up!"

Rip unrolled the chart and was studying it intently when Kawika returned with the coffee pot. Turning the up-ended cup right side up, he glanced at the second place setting. "Waitin' for the pretty lady?" His voice sounded hopeful yet guarded, as if he already knew the answer would be "no."

Rip shook his head without looking up.

"Hey, what you say to her da odder day? Musta been pretty rude ta make her run outta here like dat." His eyes twinkled. "Or did'n' she like my cookin'?"

In spite of himself, Rip smiled. "No, your cooking makes folks run *in* here, not out."

"Okay, okay! That remark gets you dinner on da house!" Kawika pulled out the other chair and plopped heavily into it. He rested his ample arms on the table, leaned forward, and said in a low voice, "now, gimme da real scoop."

Rip looked into the older man's concerned, brown face and sighed deeply. "You sure you want to hear it all? It'll take awhile."

Kawika shrugged. "Sure. Why not? Dose folks in da corner jus' about done. Weather's been so bad I'm not expectin' any rush. I go cook up your food now, den we talk story."

Rip was more hungry than he realized. Between forkfuls of perfectly browned spam, he told Kawika about Karl's plans for the resort, the argument with Jackie, and the probable loss of his boat. Kawika shook his head and made sympathetic sounds as Rip spoke. Finally, Rip explained about the visit from Kevin, and Zephyr's subsequent exposure as an environmental spy. He left for last the word "heiress."

By this time the other diners had left and Kawika had locked the door, placed the hand-lettered "closed" sign in the window, and returned to his sagging chair. Now satisfied that they would not be overheard, Rip explained his plan to disable the bulldozers and delay the destruction of the nesting site at least for the weekend.

Kawika tipped his chair back on two legs. It creaked and wobbled dangerously, but he seemed not to notice. He nibbled his bottom lip and studied the grass matting on the ceiling. Rip waited. He knew from experience that Kawika did not like to be interrupted while he was deep in thought. Finally, the big man leaned forward, planting his forearms solidly on the table and slamming the chair's front legs onto the floor with a crunching thud.

"I got it, Bro!"

"Got what?"

"Da answer to how you gonna stop Karl, dat human kudzu, and have the double-crossing lil' wahine help you do it."

"I don't need any help from her!"

"Quiet!" Kawika raised one hand for silence. "Jus' eat yer spam an' listen."

Rip's eyes widened. He stopped chewing and looked silently and expectantly at Kawika.

"Now you said she's workin' for da tree huggers, right?"

"Well, yeah, sort of."

"An' dere da ones can make lotta bad press for ol' Karl, right?"

"Sure but--"

"No 'buts.' Jus' listen. You take her wiff you tonight. Get her dat night vision camera you showed me at da shop."

"That's Jackie's. I can't --"

Kawika grinned widely. "Eben better. So you take dat pretty liddle . . . uh . . .dat two face girl with you. You have her film da beach, da turtles layin' da eggs, da bulldozers . . . better leave out da part 'bout you fixin' da dozers . . .Yeah, leave out dat part. Then she email it all to her organization an' to da TV stations."

He leaned back, looking pleased with himself. Rip was shaking his head, but Kawika took no notice.

"She get what she want, you get what you want, an' us locals get to keep our island da way it 'sposed ta be. Ever' body happy 'cept ol' Karl da Kudzu . . . " He gazed up at the ceiling, grinning so widely that all of the empty tooth sockets were revieled.. "An' maybe ol' Jackie."

Rip looked at him admiringly. The guy was smart, no question. Creative. It would have been a perfect solution except . . . "It's too dangerous for her. She's not an experienced diver. I can't put her in a situation like that."

Kawika shrugged his massive shoulders. "Jus' ask her. She kin always say no."

■ ■ ■

Zephyr snatched her yellow bikini off the hook on the back of the bathroom door, wadded it into a damp ball, and threw it into the suitcase which lay open in the center of the bed. After changing into jeans and a pink tee shirt, her travel standbys, she jerked the bureau drawers open and snatched out tee shirts, shorts, and the gauzy white cotton dress that she'd worn that night in the cemetery. The night of that first kiss.

In the books she'd read during all those lonely days on her father's sailboat, the first kiss was always followed by a "happily ever after" scene. What an idiot she'd been to believe in such rot! In the real world a kiss meant nothing. It carried no promise of anything more. To Rip she was just one more tourist, here for a few days and then gone. Two months from now he probably wouldn't even remember her name except, of course, if she followed through with her assignment even without filmed supporting evidence. Then he would remember her name all too well. The air would be turning blue around the name "Zephyr" whenever he spoke of her.

It was obvious he had never cared about her. If he had, could he have turned so suddenly cold as they left the boat this afternoon? Could he have dismissed her so easily tonight without even giving her a chance to explain her deception? He was probably just glad to have an excuse to break off their relationship without all the bother of making false promises to call or write. From her awkward high school days, she'd known that no one would ever want her, not really. She never knew the right things to say. What came so easily to other girls was a mystery to her. The years on the boat had taught her only how to talk to turtles and seabirds, not to boys.

The ugly muu-muu hanging on a hook on the back of the bathroom door caught her eye. She moved quickly across the room and yanked it down. After using it to dab at her eyes, she tossed it in the general direction of the wastebasket. She would go home, sell the furniture and the house with all the unhappy memories, find an apartment somewhere, and devote herself to writing about the environment. Maybe she could even find a volunteer position at Ocean Observers' headquarters in San Francisco. That is, if they would have her after she failed at her assignment here.

At least she had accomplished one thing. She had ended her relationship with Kevin. It had been a mistake from the beginning. Now she could see that. The intense passion she had felt for Rip made that clear. She had never felt anything even remotely like it with Kevin. He was just *there*. He was a handy cure for her fear of being alone. So now her "happily ever after" would have to come from inside herself, from doing something meaningful with her life.

She was snapping her suitcase shut when she heard a knock on the door. Assuming it was the bellboy, she called out, "come on in!"

"Okay . . . if you're not sending any secret messages on your Junior Spy Wrist Radio. Wouldn't want to interrupt a hard working mole."

That voice! She whirled around. It was the voice she had thought she would never hear again. His tall form filled the doorway. Zephyr's throat constricted squeezing her breath, making her gasp.

"Rip!" she croaked. She tried to lick her parched lips, but her mouth was suddenly as dry as that night on the boat when she hadn't been able to summon up enough spit to clear her mask.

"Can I come in? I've got a proposition for you." He was trying for a light tone, but it wasn't working. His voice got caught somewhere. He cleared his throat and coughed softly, then stepped inside.

"Yes . . . of course . . . what?" She gestured toward a wicker chair, but he remained standing, carefully closing the door behind him. Zephyr tried in vain to read his face, but in the lighted room he appeared as impassive as he had in the darkened shop. His manner was all military. He looked every inch the combat hardened SEAL.

"How would you like a real scoop for your organization's magazine? A chance to film a mega scale ecological crime rather than just going after small fish like Jackie and me?"

Every molecule in Zephyr's body longed to press itself against him, but she held herself firmly in check, trying to make her face as expressionless as his.

Jackie and me.

Did the pairing imply that they really were more than just business partners? Had that been the reason for his coldness after the return voyage? Maybe he realized that his attentions to her were a threat to his relationship with Jackie. Too much of a threat to risk. That must have been it, just as she'd guessed. She turned away from Rip and back to her suitcase, snapping it shut.

"Why are you asking me? Why don't you and Jackie just--"

He cleared his throat again. "You asked me to trust you a while ago." Combing his fingers through his hair, he gazed up at the fan blades spinning themselves into one almost invisible blur. "Okay, so now I'm asking for *your* trust. If you really care about saving turtles, you'll listen to what I have to say."

Zephyr straightened up and turned back toward him. He dropped his eyes to meet hers. "Or are you so determined to write me in as the bad guy that you are going to let the big story get away?"

Their eyes locked. They stared at each other for a full minute. Zephyr's thoughts raced in circles. After all he never implied that what they had shared was anything more than a temporary dalliance, one of those beach-boy-and-tourist kinds of things. Now I've done it again. I've been too unsophisticated . . . too . . . she struggled against bringing the hated word into consciousness . . . too vulnerable. How foolish I was to believe that I meant something to him! The only evidence for that was just wishful thinking.

Well, no more!

From now on she'd be the hardened lady journalist and environmental cop that she'd always fantasized being.

Maybe she wouldn't have to go home without accomplishing anything. He was throwing her a challenge, a chance for the Big Story, the Big Bust. What if he *had* just been amusing himself with her? Now it was her turn to use him..

"Sure." She was relieved to hear her voice come out tough and strong. "What 'big story' do you have in mind?"

"I'll have to show you." Without taking his eyes off of her, he turned the doorknob. "But you'll have to come back to the dive shop with me. He held the door open for her adding casually, "Oh . . . and bring your swimsuit."

Zephyr stepped back to where the suitcase lay firmly closed on the bed. She hugged her arms tightly, sighed deeply, and reluctantly opened it again.

■ ■ ■

They walked in silence towards the dive shop, Rip a little ahead, Zephyr hurrying to keep up while her dive bag prodded her leg. The strolling crowds had thinned out now. Just one couple, lovers with eyes only for each other, passed them. Zephyr tried not to allow herself to conjure up images of herself and Rip running hand in hand down this very street, side by side in the rain. Could it really have been only two days ago?

Rip unlocked the front door of the shop and they stepped inside. He crossed the squeaking wooden floor quickly with his long stride. In the dim light, wetsuits hung like decapitated bodies from their hangers on a round rack. Zephyr winced as a rubbery sleeve brushed against her. Stepping behind the counter, Rip clicked on the lights and instantly they were facing each other across a glass case filled with knives, waterproof watches, and cheap disposable underwater cameras. His expression remained impassively neutral as he unrolled a chart that had been lying on the counter. He smoothed it with both hands and spread it out between them.

"Okay, here's the deal," he said. "I learned today that this weekend there is going to be an attempt to wipe out the most unspoiled turtle nesting site on the island."

Zephyr gasped. "But why? Why would anyone--"

Rip raised one eyebrow. "You mean you don't know? I thought you were the environmental expert."

She considered the situation for a moment. "Oh yeah. Now I get it. Someone plans to do something with that beach and doesn't want to have to put up with governmental regulations about the use of endangered species habitat. So whoever it is just quickly gets rid of--"

"The evidence. Exactly. But tonight I'm going to stop them by disabling the bulldozers. Of course that's only temporary. They'll fix them on Monday morning What I need is someone with your contacts and . . . uhh . . . covert ops experience--"

Sarcasm or dry humor?

". . . to film the beach and the nesting site as evidence of this . . . this environmental crime. When Karl sees we've got proof of what he's up to, I'm betting he backs off in a hurry."

"Karl?"

"Jackie's father. The guy I told you about who builds those posh resorts."

"Oh, that Karl."

"Yeah." Rip's mouth was set in a tight, grim line.

"But what does Jackie say about this? Won't she be mad at you?" Zephyr felt a nudge of optimism gathering.

"I certainly hope so." He gave a short laugh. "But let's get back to planning. We have a long night ahead of us."

Zephyr felt lighter than she had all day. She wanted to quiz him further, but realized this probably wasn't the time. Later.

Rip slid his finger over the chart tracing a route from the spot marked, *Turtle Beach*. "We could just go straight in from the boat, swimming underwater with air tanks, but that would mean having to walk out of the water and up the beach in plain sight. Unfortunately, tonight we've got a full moon, so not only could they see us, but they could see the boat anchored off shore as well."

"They?"

He gave her a withering look. "Some spy you are. You don't think Karl'd just leave the 'dozers for anyone to find, do you? He's sure to have sent in his security guards. Probably armed, too."

"Can't we just slip in from land? Through the bushes?"

"Bushes? You mean jungle." With his hand, he made a swirling motion above the chart indicating most of the land area shown. "This m'dear is not covered with ornamental shrubbery. The bulldozers will have carved a path, but you can bet it's well patrolled. Besides it would take too long to get there through that rough country . . . steep valleys . . . cliffs. We haven't got that kind of time."

"Soo . . . what's your plan?"

He placed both of his hands on the counter and leaned forward looking sharply into her face. "The turtle cave."

"What?" She felt a swelling wave of nausea, but looked unwaveringly back at him.

"You remember how on our night dive I warned everyone not to go too far into the cave?"

"I think so . . . yes, I remember. You said it was a lava tube and it led to a remote part of the island."

Rip gave a short laugh. "If Karl has his way it won't be remote for long. Next year at this time It'll be crawling with people instead of baby turtles."

She gave him a wicked smile. "I seem to remember someone saying something about the needs of people having to be taken into account."

He winced. "Okay, okay. Needs . . . wants . . ." His eyes slid away from hers.

"Like I told you, it's a complicated question, but maybe I've mostly seen one side . . ." His dimple made a brief appearance, flashing in his cheek to accompany an ironic half-grin. ". . . the side that was useful to me, of course." Shifting his gaze back to her, his voice turned hard again. "But now we've got work to do, working for the animals' side this time, so let's argue animal rights later, okay?"

They stared at each other over the unrolled page, then she nodded briefly. "Okay. Now what about the lava tube?"

He drew his finger across the chart tracing an imaginary line from the turtle cave anchorage over the top of a ridge and ending at a point on the far side of it. "This is where the lava tube comes out. Do you know what I mean when I say 'lava tube'?"

Reluctantly, she shook her head.

"Well, lava tubes aren't exactly caves in the sense of Mainland caves. They are channels through which lava flowed during the time after the ground at the surface cooled and hardened. The lava kept flowing and gas created hollows. Thus, 'lava tube' or we can just call it a cave."

"So that's how we are getting to the turtle beach. Then what?"

"We'll approach through the cave and that way you can photograph from the shelter of the rocks near the opening without being observed. Meanwhile, I'll be disabling the dozers. My black wetsuit should act as camouflage if I can keep to the shadows."

"Will there be enough light for the camera?"

He lifted one finger. "Hang on." Removing a key from a loop on his belt, he unlocked the sliding back door of the glass case and pulled out a camcorder that looked like a cell phone. "Infrared. It's waterproof, but infrared doesn't work very well underwater so we haven't done much with it, but it will work fine for photographing the beach and the turtles. It will automatically stamp the time and date. That's important."

Zephyr took it from his hand. It was small but heavier than she expected. She examined it, quickly familiarizing herself with the operation. It looked pretty easy.

Rip took it back saying, "just a second." He bent down and rummaged through a drawer and when he returned the camera to her, it had a sturdy neck strap attached. "Seeing as it's you, we'd better bring this." He looped the strap over her head.

"*Seeing as it's you* . . ." Losing a camera in the ocean could have happened to anyone. Why did he have to remind her in that patronizing way?

She glared at him, but he wasn't looking at her. He had turned his attention back to the chart. With his finger, he indicated a point of land just to the north of the beach. "What we'll do is anchor off Alai Point here. The boat will be out of sight behind the cliff. We'll go down the anchor line and swim in along the bottom. It's shallow, only about thirty feet. Normally when we take divers to the cave we anchor out farther because I don't like to take them that close to the rocks. This time, though, we'll need to save our air supply to get through the tunnel then back out after we finish the operation."

An electric ripple surged across Zephyr's scalp. She was back again on the sailboat anchored at Tonga Tapu.

"Trust me. It's only a short tunnel. Just dive down, swim hard and you'll pop up inside the cave where there's an air pocket. Only takes a few seconds. You can hold your breath that long!" "No Daddy. I can't do it! I'm scared."

Her father's frowning face loomed in her memory.

" . . . Earth to Zephyr . . . I said, 'do you think you can do it?'" Rip was staring at her, no doubt measuring her courage, her determination.

Zephyr swallowed hard. "Sure. No problem."

10

Moonlight ignited a path of shimmering silver across the blackness of the sea. Reflected light from the surface of the water returned the brilliance to the sky causing it to glow a magical deep blue. Rip, at the wheel of the *Ipo Nui*, glanced down at Zephyr where she sat in the first mate's chair. "Warm enough?"

"I'm fine, thank you." She was relieved to hear her words come out with just the right degree of impersonal politeness.

"Okay. Good." He checked the GPS on the instrument panel. "It's about time to get suited up. You can change in my cabin."

"Okay. Thank you." She stood, steady despite the bounding of the boat, then swung herself down the steep ladder to the main deck. After taking a moment to allow herself to be swept up in the beauty of the night, she descended four more steps making her way through the outer cabin then opening the door into Rip's private quarters. She snapped on the light. Over the roar of the engines, she could distinctly hear a tiny "meow." Looking in the direction of the sound she saw something that melted the ice which had been forming around her heart all afternoon. There, in the middle of Rip's quilt covered bunk, was a curled, furry shape. It was the black and white kitten from Kawika's.

A half-empty bowl of cat food on the floor gave mute testimony to the kitten's improved life style. Zephyr smiled. In two quick steps, she crossed the space between the door and the bunk and perched on its edge. She picked the kitten up and cuddled it.

"So . . . Mr. Cat, now we know that Captain Tough Guy is really a marshmallow, don't we?" The kitten answered with a loud purr.

■ ■ ■

Returning to the bridge a few minutes later, with her bikini under the heavy gauge wetsuit Rip had brought for her from the shop, Zephyr didn't mention the kitten. Something told her that now was not the right time. Later they could talk about it when they returned from Turtle Beach -- *if* they returned. Her stomach fluttered at the thought of swimming into that dark cave again.

Rip cut the engine power. The *Ipo Nui* sank down into the undulating waves and began to float slowly toward a rocky headland. Zephyr's chest grew tight. The wetsuit seemed to be squeezing her like a boa constrictor as the headland became a black shadow looming above them.

"Okay, close enough." Rip spoke in clipped tones. "Here, take the helm while I set the anchor."

He was gone before she had time to protest. What gave him the right to bark orders at her? The wheel was cold in her hands.

Then quickly she felt the lurch and pull of the anchor taking hold. It was time to put on the tanks. Quivering, she descended the ladder to the main deck. The bridge was empty now. There was no one at the helm. If they ran into trouble there was no one to come to their aid. No one knew they were there. No one would miss them for hours . . . maybe days.

Zephyr's mouth felt like cotton. She didn't even try to spit into her dive mask, just silently accepted the bottle of mask defogger that Rip handed to her.

"Do you remember how to work the camera?" He placed it in her gloved hand and looped its strap over her head.

She nodded, hoping she did.

Silently, they slipped into their inflatable dive vests and helped each other turn on the air valves to their tanks. Together they stepped out onto the platform at the stern of the boat. Zeph staggered, bending awkwardly at the waist to compensate for the weight of the tank on her back.

"Easy." Rip steadied her with one hand under her elbow. She wanted to shake him off. She wanted to show him she could take care of herself. Instead she found herself pressed against his reassuring solidness by the motion of the sea.

"Ready?" he asked almost gently.

She nodded, not trusting herself to speak lest her words become a scream of protest.

"All right then . . . " He put his thumb and forefinger together in the "okay" signal. "To the rescue of Mother Nature!" He slapped the regulator into his mouth and jumped feet first into the water.

Zephyr hesitated until she saw the gleam of reflected moonlight on his mask. He was back on the surface waiting for her. She stepped forward and was instantly engulfed in cold, black water. Fighting hysteria, her head swiveled in all directions until she glimpsed the beam of his dive light carving a tiny tunnel through the total darkness of the water. Kicking hard, she followed him downward. The water grew colder.

They had been swimming for only a few minutes when she felt a heavy swell begin to rock her. It took all her strength to maintain a straight course behind Rip. She glared at his light bobbing in front of her. Had he forgotten that she was not as strong a swimmer as he was?

Turn around, damn you! Look at me!

She wanted to shout at him to slow down, to wait for her, but she knew that the sound would not carry far under water. Even more important, she needed to keep her teeth clamped on the regulator in order to suck its precious air.

Then she had a sense of the water above her boiling and churning. It must be the waves beating against the cliff face. Unexpectedly, surge smashed her against a sharp rock. She thrust out her left hand, reflexively guarding the camera, and mumbled an "ouch" into the regulator as the backwash sucked her away.

As if he had heard, Rip turned and shown the light on her. Quickly he was by her side, his big hand clamped around her wrist pulling her forward. The tumultuous water went suddenly still. Except for the feeble glow of the dive light, the blackness was absolute. She knew what that meant. It meant they were inside the cave.

"Daddy, no! I don't want to!"

"Take a big breath and trust me . . . trust me . . . "

The pressure in Zeph's ears told her they were going deeper. She pinched her nose with the fingers of her free hand, blew air into her ear canals and heard the welcome snap. The pressure eased.

As the tunnel narrowed, Rip was forced to release her and swim ahead. Then, without warning, there was a disturbance in the water. A huge dark shape rushed above them. It was followed by another, and another. The turtles! They were so close that the foot of one of them caught briefly in Zephyr's hair as it passed above her. She felt a moment of panic, then remembered that the creatures were more scared than she was. And for better reasons.

Focus! They are the ones in danger here! We are the intruders.

The tunnel widened. A ghostly blue light surrounded them. Zephyr felt herself being drawn upwards by her natural buoyancy. Her head popped out of the water and warm air touched her face. Rip surfaced in front of her, his head and shoulders above the water. He spat out his regulator. "Save your air. You can breathe in here. Let's rest for a few minutes on this ledge."

As her eyes became accustomed to the strange half-light, Zeph could see the rocky ceiling a few feet above them. Rip lifted himself onto a ledge then offered his hand to pull her up. She handed him the camera then scrambled up unaided.

"Where . . . what is this?" She turned and sat, letting her regulator fall onto her chest, and taking a big breath of the stale musty air.

"Blowhole." Rip pointed toward the ceiling with his thumb. "Low tide now, so it's quiet." He looked at his watch. "In a couple of hours, though, it'll be a raging hell in here. Water gets compressed by the waves and shoots out through that hole."

Zephyr looked upwards. Sure enough. She could see a ragged slit less than a foot wide, letting in silvery moonlight. "But . . . but we have to come back through . . ." Her voice trailed off.

He patted her knee with his gloved hand. "Take it easy. I've got it timed so we'll be long gone by high tide. You're with a pro, remember?"

She snapped her mask up onto her forehead and gave him what she intended to be a doubtful look. He didn't seem to notice.

"So," he said without preamble, "Do you want to tell me who ratted us out? Or is that information classified?"

Zephyr caught one fingertip of her glove between her teeth and pulled it off. Her hands always felt smothered in gloves.

"Well?" he said.

"'Well' what?"

"How did you find out about the turtle riding?" His voice was calm, patient.

Perhaps she did owe him an explanation, just as she had owed Kevin.

"We got an anonymous letter."

"Ah, yes. Good old Mr. Anonymous. You can always count on him for a knife in the back. Or was it her? Was it Ms Anonymous?"

"I really couldn't say." Her voice was as distant as she could make it in such close quarters.

"Couldn't, or won't?"

"Can't because I don't know. The organization that I work for, Ocean Observers, got the letter. That's all they told me. They were looking for someone with scuba diving experience to check it out, so they called me."

He leaned forward to peer into her face. "And what made them think you had scuba experience?"

She looked away. "I did. They sent a skills inventory and I checked 'certified scuba diver.'" She snapped her head back to face him. "Well, I am!"

He lifted one eyebrow. "Sure. Certified to rescue band aids from pool drains."

As she struggled for a haughty reply, Zephyr felt the corners of her mouth twitch with what was threatening to become a smile. She stifled it quickly.

Rip stirred the water with his fin. "And may I ask one thing before you turn me over to the environmentalist mob to be drawn and quartered?"

"What do you want to know?"

He put both hands on her shoulders and, turning her towards him, looked her hard in the face. "Why didn't you just tell me straight out who you were and why you were here?"

She felt her face flush. Under her wet hair her scalp grew hot. "And if I had?"

"If you'd been honest with me from the beginning, you would have learned that I'd expressly forbidden Jackie to touch those turtles."

"But she didn't listen to you."

He dropped his hands and looked away. "No. You're right. She didn't."

"Was she really that desperate for customers?"

He sighed heavily. "I thought so. It turns out to be not quite that simple, though. Seems she had herself convinced she was doing the turtles a favor."

"A favor? How?"

"She knew what her father was up to. That he wanted to get rid of the nesting grounds so he wouldn't have to deal with any restrictions on his resort development. She thought she could scare them away." He kicked at the water with both fins. "At least that's what she told me."

Zephyr nodded. "And when she told you . . . ?"

"That's when I told her our partnership was over even through it's going to cost me my boat."

She said nothing for a moment. So whatever had been between him and Jackie, it was over. But his boat was his business, his home, his dream, his life. "I'm sorry," she said softly.

"Yeah, well . . . " He looked at her and grinned suddenly. "I'm not. I will have to start over but it's worth it to be free of Karl and his money. I can go back to scraping the bottoms of other people's boats. It may take a while, but I can save up enough to begin again."

"Do you think there's any chance we could talk to Karl? Get him to scale down the resort? Save some beach for the turtles? Ecotourism, maybe?"

Rip's tank clanged against the wall of the cave as he leaned back. He gazed upward at the slot of moonlight. "Let me tell you about Karl. Karl is so greedy that when he was a kid, he set a trap for the tooth fairy, baited it with a nice big molar, and planned to hold her hostage until she gave up all her silver dollars instead of giving him just one at a time."

Zeph was quiet, thinking, then she said, "Do you mean the tooth fairy gives silver dollars?"

"Sure. Yours didn't?"

"No. Sea shells."

"Hummm . . . I guess there wasn't any place for you to spend silver dollars, was there?"

"No. Besides I never cared about money anyway. It wasn't important in my life because--"

"Because you had lots of it. But you heiresses can always find something . . . or someone . . . " His voice, echoing off the damp walls, turned heavy with bitterness. " . . . to buy, to control."

Zephyr gasped and choked. *How could I have started to feel sorry for such a self-righteous jerk?* "Is that what you think of me? That I'm another control freak like Linda or Jackie?"

Rip slid forward and studied his watch.

Zephyr's heart was racing in anger. "Is it? Is that what you really think? Tell me, is it?"

In a flash he was the combat hardened SEAL again. Without a word he handed the camera back to her and snapped his mask back in place over his eyes and nose. He held his regulator in his hand. "What I think of you doesn't matter right now. We need to get moving if we're going to make it out of here ahead of the tide.. Stay close behind me and when we surface, try not to make any noise."

He moved to the edge of the rocky shelf and dropped below the water leaving scarcely a ripple to show where he had been.

For a moment, Zephyr sat unmoving. The temptation to turn around alone, to go back the way they had come was so overwhelming that it felt like a giant hand dragging her. Instantly she was back in the remote island in the South Pacific where her father had bullied and taunted her into following him into a cave with an underwater entrance.

"Trust me."

Her father had learned free diving from the islanders. Strapping on a "bubbling, clumsy air tank" was not his style.

"Listen Zeph, I taught you to swim by dropping you in a pool. You're going to learn to dive the same way. There's an air filled cave at the end of the tunnel, but you've got to hold your breath long enough to get to it. You can do it. Don't be a sissy!"

Finally she had tried, really tried, but in the darkness she had panicked. With barely enough air in her small lungs to make it out, she had turned back. She'd earned her father's scorn when what she most wanted was his respect.

Oh sure, she knew now what he'd done was risky and abusive. She knew it, but still the shame burned. After all, he was her father.

But now she was an adult with a job to do. This was only one beach, but habitats all over the world were being lost . . . one at a time. What they were trying to do here was to save just one nesting site, yet without it the world would be a poorer place. She slipped the camera strap over her head and stuck her regulator in her mouth, clearing it with one sharp breath. Then she slid off the ledge into the blackness below.

Rip was waiting for her, hanging just below the surface She sensed his presence even before he switched on his dive light. He aimed the beam at his hand and gave her the okay sign along with a questioning look barely visible behind his mask.

When she had returned the sign as confirmation that she was, at least for the moment, okay, Rip turned and began to kick deeper into the enveloping darkness.

Zephyr followed his fins staying as close as she safely could. Even at that range it was hard to keep his light in view. Particles swirling in the water diffused and dimmed it. The muscles of her thighs began to cramp, but she forced herself to keep moving. Rip might be a self-righteous jerk, but if she let any distance grow between them she could be lost in here blundering down dead ends, trapped in tight corners. She'd be lost forever . . . or at least until she ran out of air, sucking desperately on the empty regulator. Above her not air, but solid rock. Lost even in death, because most likely no one would ever even find her body. Nausea gripped her at the thought.

Inside her head, she heard a remembered voice. "*. . .above all, don't panic . . .* "

Whose voice? On that first night dive it had been Kevin's. This time, so clearly that she couldn't deny it, it was Rip's... .

"*. . . the opposite of fear is trust . . . trust your buddy . . . *"

Trust your buddy? Right now it was all she could do to keep up with him. If she fell behind, if she got lost, how long before he would notice?

Turn around, dammit! Wait for me!

If he could have heard her underwater, she would have been tempted to scream the words even through it would have meant losing her mouthpiece. But she knew he couldn't hear and she knew he couldn't turn around. There wasn't room. She felt, rather than saw, the walls of the tunnel closing in on them. She was terrifyingly aware of the bulky tank on her back, solid like a turtle shell. What if it were to catch on an overhanging rock, trapping her?

No! Don't think! Just keep moving! The only way out of this is through it. Got to control the fear. Racing heart uses too much oxygen.

She forced herself to take long, slow breaths. Too her surprise and relief, the very act of calming her breathing, calmed her fear as well. She was just beginning to relax when Rip's light flickered once, then disappeared.

The darkness was complete again.

Terror, like a physical blow, rushed through her. Her thigh muscles screamed out for rest, but there was nowhere to go except forward.

Just keep kicking.

It seemed like forever, alone in the dark, until her head broke the surface of the water. A cool evening breeze ruffled her wet hair. Rip was gripping her hand and pulling her up onto the rocks. As she tipped her face back and snapped her mask up onto her forehead, her gaze was met by open sky -- the blessed sky and stars.

When she relaxed her aching jaw and let go of the regulator, she was free to take a deep, wonderful breath, but when she tried to rise from her kneeling position, she found she could not. The weight of the tank on her back was too great.

"Stay low." She was relieved to hear Rip's calm whisper.

"Sure. No problem," she hissed, "since I can't stand up with this tank on my back anyhow."

"I'll take it off and stash it over there with mine under that rock ledge.

As quietly as possible she unsnapped the buckles at her waist and chest and pulled off her fins. Gratefully, she felt Rip lift the weight of the tank off of her but she stayed on her knees. Crawling, she followed Rip's bent over dark shape a few feet to an indentation in the rocks that loomed before them. A small hollow had been carved there during centuries of high tides. Now it was a dry refuge. Rip placed her tank next to his and they both slipped into a sandy pocket behind them. For the first time since they left the boat, she felt safe. The dark was no longer a threat. It had become a sheltering friend.

But horror quickly replaced relief. There was a sound of snapping branches and the thud of boots hitting the ground. Rip seized her, covering her mouth with his hand. His big fingers forced her lips against her teeth.

"Shhh!" His mouth was pressed against her ear. She could feel his breath. They crouched together like one body, their breathing synchronized without conscious intent.

A two-way radio crackled out unintelligible words. Terrifyingly close, a gruff voice replied, "Conners here. Go ahead."

Zephyr's eyes, which had squeezed shut as Rip grabbed her, opened to see the dim outline of a pair of dark-clad legs. The rest of the body was hidden behind a rock outcropping.

The radio crackled again. Zephyr strained to hear the words coming from it. Perhaps there would be some clue about where the security guard, this Conners guy, was to go next -- hopefully far from here. She listened so hard that she could almost feel her ears stretch forward like a cat's. But she heard only a rough, muffled male voice. The words were unclear.

Rip softened his hold on her mouth, yet he continued to press her close to him. His body covered hers. His arm around her waist clutched her into the hollow of his chest. Even through their wetsuits, she could feel the deep, steady beat of his heart. She was shocked to feel her body respond in a way that, given their predicament, was wildly inappropriate.

"Uh huh . . . sure . . . " The harsh voice above them mumbled his end of the conversation. "Yeah . . . will do. When? . . . . well, ahh . . . what's your twenty? . . . . be right there . . . "

Rip's hand, which had been guarding her mouth, slid away from her lips. His strong fingers cupped her cheek with astonishing gentleness. She felt her breathing slow as she swallowed a sigh that might have betrayed them.

". . . over and out."

She saw a disembodied hand reach down from above and adjust his pants. With a frisson of fright, she recognized that the vague shape hanging beside his leg was a very large gun.

He could shoot us! But he's through talking. Surely he'll leave now.

The hand disappeared but the legs did not move. There was a rustling sound followed quickly by the scratch and flare of a match. The big feet in their thick-soled boots shuffled. Conners made a smacking sound. He must have taken a deep draw on a cigarette, because she could smell smoke.

Oh no! Smoke makes me sneeze!

She concentrated on taking tiny breaths through her mouth.

The feet shuffled again and she saw the cigarette drop. It rolled towards them in slow motion. A boot moved after it and came so close that she feared he would step on her hand. The boot twisted the cigarette out. Sand flew in her eyes. She blinked rapidly.

Finally, with one last shuffle accompanied by a harsh cough from their owner, the feet stomped away. Rip's hand tightened its grip on her waist in a silent warning not to move too soon.

Gradually the crunch of footsteps faded into the distance and was covered by the lapping sound of surf against the beach.

"Good job!" Rip whispered in her ear. "I'll make a SEAL out of you yet!"

She felt a warm glow spread out from the center of her body. For a brief moment she nearly forgot their precarious situation.

"Okay, now stay low." He released her and gradually began to move as he spoke. "We're going to crawl out and do a quick recon. When I give you the signal, you can start filming. Be sure to get the name on the side of the 'dozers. After that, turn your camera on the edge of the water. Got it?"

She nodded, then unsure if he could see her, she whispered back, "Got it."

He gave her a quick pat on the shoulder and was gone, vanishing so suddenly and silently that it took a moment for her to comprehend the fact that she was alone. Alone except for Conners. Wherever he was.

Lacking the shelter of Rip's body, Zephyr began to feel a chill. Out of the water the wetsuit radiated heat away from her body. It held her in a clammy embrace which she longed to shed, but she knew that the suit's dark exterior provided better camouflage than her too white skin. At least she could get rid of the clumsy gloves. She pulled them off with her teeth and left them next to her tank in the hollow.

With her newly freed fingers, she grabbed the camera and brushed sand off the case. She lifted it into position. Through the lens of the camera, giant earth moving equipment that, to her naked eyes, had been visible only as huge shapes, stood out clearly in eerie green. She focused on the letters emblazoned on the door of the closest machine -- "King Cole Enterprises, Royal Resorts."

Zeph repressed a snuff of derision. Whatever Rip does to that guy's equipment he had it coming for that stupid pun.

After filming what she hoped was enough of the equipment, she turned the camera toward the sea. At first she saw nothing, only green water lapping greener sand. Then she noticed movement. Vague shapes like manhole covers were climbing out of the water and onto the beach.

"Turtles!

The turtles were arriving to lay their eggs. Her mission fading into the back of her mind, Zephyr watched in awe. Female turtles, half buried in the sand, dotted the beach. Still more were emerging from the water. She had to get closer! She needed to make sure that the round shapes would be clearly visible as what they were - mysterious survivors from the age of the dinosaurs, now threatened with extinction because of the greed of humans. These turtles, having traveled thousands of miles on the open ocean, had somehow found their way back to the very beach on which they had been born. It was a genuine miracle. No one, not even a self-appointed "king" had a right to destroy them.

She pulled herself on her elbows out of the shelter of the deeply shadowed rocks onto a sandy rise. It provided a good vantage point from which to zoom in on individual turtles. As soon as she was satisfied that she had evidence enough, she tucked the camera inside her wetsuit. It lay cold and hard between her breasts, but at least it was safe. She wouldn't lose this one!

Then, just as she had nearly forgotten Conners and his big gun, she heard a pop echoing off the rocks. Terror rushed in a burning wave through her. It clamped her chest so tightly she couldn't breathe. The first popping sound was followed by more and more, too many to count.

Undeniably gunshots. And they were getting closer. Where was Rip?

She flattened herself against the sand. Her heart pounded painfully. Crab-like she backed toward the shelter of the rocks as puffs of sand exploded around her. There was a dreadful pinging sound as a bullet hit something metallic.

Where is Rip? And then he was beside her and they were both rolling and clawing their way into the scooped out place below the rocks. His strong arm locked around her waist as he dragged her the last few feet.

"Hurry!" His voice was raspy. "Help me on with my tank and I'll get yours. Gotta get outta here fast!"

In a flurry of straps they helped each other into their fins and tanks then scrambled toward the pool of water at the opening of the cave. Zephyr noticed gratefully that the water was deeper and closer than it had been when they arrived. It would make their escape faster. It didn't occur to her that it would also make conditions more dangerous in the blowhole. At the moment she was just grateful that the rocks sheltered them from the flying bullets.

Zephyr reached for her regulator to pop it in her mouth, but something was wrong. Where her hand should have felt smooth metal, it found instead sharp, jagged edges and shreds of rubber. Her fear-dulled brain refused to process the unexpected information. She simply hung by one hand to an outcropping while her hand protested the rock's volcanic roughness.

Damn. Lost the gloves!

Immediately, Rip was beside her. He took the remains of the regulator from her hand then whispered an oath.

"Your regulator's gone. Hit by a bullet. We'll have to bud-dy breathe."

Buddy breathe? Like with Good Ol' Chuck?

They could hear the sound of heavy boots crunching through underbrush. It was growing closer. No choice.

Trust. The opposite of fear. *Trust me*. Ultimate trust.

Rip's arm clamped around her waist and they dropped below the surface into total darkness.

11

She could still breathe. Rip's regulator, attached by a hose to his air tank, was in her mouth. But she knew that in seconds she would have to give it up to him. She would have to trust him to pass it back. Then she would have to keep fighting terror long enough to continue taking turns until they reached the surface - on the far side of the tunnel.

If we can find our way out! She would have to trust Rip for that, too.

The darkness around them was total. She knew in a flash why Rip could not use his light while they swam. He needed to use one arm to hold them close together and the other hand to pass the regulator. If she had known where he kept his dive light, she could have turned it on. But she didn't. Besides the passage was so narrow that with the two of them side by side there wasn't room to fumble around for it. Trust again. She would have to trust that he knew the way out even in the surrounding blackness.

She felt a tug on the regulator. Reflexively, her teeth clamped down on it. But, of course, Rip needed air. She must release her hold. Now. He needed it now.

Later she would remember that relaxing her jaw at that moment was the hardest thing she'd ever done. Every nerve in her body cried out against it. Every instinct from the deepest, most primitive parts of her brain screamed *me, me, mine!* But their ribs were pressed together. She could feel his chest not moving. He was much stronger than she was. He could have yanked away the life giving air. Instead, he waited. But he couldn't hold his breath much longer. He was depending on her completely.

After a last deep gasp, she parted her teeth and let go.

His chest expanded. She could feel the relief in his body. He gave her waist a quick squeeze of gratitude even as the walls of the tunnel crushed them more closely together. They were surrounded on all sides by unyielding rock. At that moment, she had no air but what was left inside her lungs.

This must be what it's like to be buried alive!

And then Rip was pressing the regulator against her mouth. She clamped her teeth on it and drew in the wonderful air that still held the taste of his lips. Two rapid inhales and she pushed the mouthpiece away with her tongue. She didn't need to hang on. He would return it. She knew that now.

Trust. That's how it feels to trust.

They fell into a smooth rhythm of passing the mouthpiece back and forth between them. Gradually the passage widened and Rip was pulling her upward. Their heads finally broke the surface of the water. Zephyr blinked. They were bathed in silvery moonlight reflected by splashing water. It lighted the cave around them. They were back in the blowhole. Now they could let go of the regulator and breathe real air. Now they were safe. Maybe they could just stay here, with light and non-compressed air, until morning.

But as Rip hauled her up onto the same rock ledge where they'd rested before, Zeph noticed that something was different.

"In a couple of hours . . . a raging hell . . . "

The ledge was almost underwater. High tide was approaching.

"Are you okay?" Rip slid her mask up onto her forehead after doing the same with his own. He gazed anxiously into her eyes.

"Fine. I'm fine. Are you?

His fingers laced through her wet hair. He pressed her face against his shoulder. "I am now. If I'd gotten you hurt, I'd never have forgiven myself."

"Gotten you hurt? Excuse me?" She looked up at him. "Gotten you hurt? It was my choice to come here!" She sat up straight, her smile softening her words.

"Hey, hey . . . " His voice was gentle. "Take it easy. That wasn't some kind of chauvinist put down. I just meant that this - tonight - was my idea. Okay?" He tilted her chin up with his fingertips then, before she had time to speak, he pressed his lips hard against hers. Their tongues found each other as the kiss deepened. The cave, the rising water, the close call they'd had, floated out of her consciousness as if it had been a bad dream. Nothing existed at that moment except him and his body so close and so strong beside her.

A wave rushed in reminding Rip of their precarious situation. He released her, but in the eerie, flickering pool of moonlight reflecting off the water, she glimpsed intense emotion in his eyes. Was it respect? Was it, perhaps, even . . . love?

"Zephyr, you were great back there!" Both of his hands clasped her shoulders as he gave her a little congratulatory shake. It was the sort of embrace guys give each other when their team has scored a goal. "We've got to get out of here fast, but I want you to know that you're as good a dive buddy as I've ever had. What we did back there takes total trust between partners and you came through superbly. You are one tough cookie!"

He took one hand from her shoulder and gave her a light slap on the thigh. An image of football players on TV flashed through her mind. Had the kiss been simply gratitude? An adrenaline rush?

He released the other shoulder and pawed through the pockets of his dive vest finally producing his dive light. Clicking it on, he directed the beam onto his air gauge.

"Just what I was afraid of. My air's almost gone. We'll both have to use yours since we don't have enough space or time in here to switch tanks. I'll take off your trashed regulator and put my operational one on yours."

He clicked off the light and stuck it back in his pocket, then grabbed her shoulders again and turned her so fast she almost lost her balance. She might have fallen off the ledge if he hadn't been holding her. Over the increasing roar of the water she could hear the clicks of the valves as he uncoupled and exchanged hoses and mouthpieces behind the back of her neck.

Even in the patchy light, Zephyr was terribly aware that the water which had been calm on their passage in, was now rocking and ricocheting in the enclosed space.

She could hear it crashing against the walls. She winced as drops splattered her face.

After giving the equipment on her back a final tug to make sure all connections were tight, Rip leaned over her shoulder. Hoping she could hear him above the rising whoosh of the waves, he shouted, "now you're the one with the air. If you want to go off and leave me, you and the turtles can have the last laugh."

"I thought you said something about total tr--" Her words were cut off by a violent surge of water that lifted them off the ledge and smashed them into the jagged rocks of the cave's ceiling. Zephyr's mouth was filled with the harsh taste of salt. She grabbed for her mask but it was gone. Rolling and tumbling, she clutched at the water, struggling for the surface with no idea where the surface was. Churning water was everywhere. It burned her eyes, her nose, her throat. Frantically, she clawed the water, searching for her regulator mouthpiece. Had Rip completed the transfer in time? If they lost the one functioning regulator they were both as good as dead.

And then her fingertips, raw from the sharp rocks, found the regulator mouthpiece. It was thrashing at the end of its rubber hose. She grabbed it and, with a silent prayer of thanks, stuck it between her teeth clearing it free of water with the last puff of air left in her lungs. But where was Rip? They'd been swept of the ledge together. The roiling water must have yanked them apart.

Rip! Where are you? Rip!

Without her mask she was blind underwater. Even the flashes of moonlight were no help. She started kicking hoping her outstretched hands would contact the familiar firmness of his body, but she felt nothing except the horrible, lonely emptiness of water.

With a sickening thud, her head hit the wall of the blowhole. She had only an instant to think -- *You do see stars! Just like in the comic books!* Then she realized that she was being sucked outward by the retreating wave.

Of course! The water would find the way out and it would pull Rip with her!

She was spinning out of control, helpless in the power of the current, when he was dashed against her, his big body limp. Without a second thought, she yanked the regulator from her own mouth and thrust it into his, pressing his lips around it. If he had even a bit of breath left in his lungs, he could clear the mouthpiece and draw in some life-giving air. But he was so horribly limp! He didn't seem to be conscious. There was just one chance . . . She cocked her free hand back and socked him as hard as she could just below the rib cage.

There was no sound but the rushing water.

Come on, Rip! Please!

She struck him again using all the strength her exhausted body could muster. And then she heard the blessed whoosh of exhaled air. Bubbles shot out of the regulator. Ignoring her own bursting lungs, she continued to press his mouth against the regulator until she heard two inhalations. Only then, when she was in danger of blacking out herself, did she suck a quick breath holding her face cheek to cheek with his.

Blind in the rush of water, she clung to him as the retreating wave carried them outward. Overwhelming relief filled her, sang through her. But it was short lived. An incoming surge thrust them back again -- back towards the deeper darkness, back toward the booming, roaring surf inside the blowhole. The inward pressure tried to tear Rip away from her. She clutched wildly at him in a terrible tug-of-war with the sea. If she lost him now there was no hope for him. By the time she could find him and give him more air, it would be too late.

Then, just as she felt him slipping away, her hand caught in his weight belt. She kicked hard giving herself enough momentum to slip her entire forearm underneath the belt. Locked against her side, he was safe as long as the buckle held. Biting hard on the mouthpiece to keep it in place, her free hand groped wildly for something -- anything to hold onto. If she could fight the inward surge, then ride the retreating waves, they had a chance.

Rocks slashed her fingers then the current slid her away. She had to have a moment to pass the regulator back to him, but she couldn't spare either hand. Frantically, she kicked again and heard a metallic clang as her tank bashed into unyeilding rock. They were caught against an outcropping in the side of the cave. The water had pushed them into one of the alcoves where the turtles rested.

Of course!

It was so simple she couldn't imagine why it hadn't occurred to her sooner. Keep to the sides of the tunnel. Move gradually out -- forward on the retreating wave then catch in a turtle hole when the water raced back. This was what the turtles had learned from eons of adaptation. It was one more glimpse of the miracles of nature.

She took a quick breath then pressed the regulator into Rip's mouth. Unprotected without her mask, her eyes burned sharply from the salt water, but she ignored the pain. Right now only one thing mattered - getting Rip to fresh air. Getting them both out before the air tank on her back was empty.

It seemed like forever. Ride the waves out. Kick hard to stay against the side of the tunnel until they were pushed into an alcove. Stay in the alcove as the water raced in. Use the interval to breathe. Ride the retreating water out farther.

And finally -- casting a glow even under the water -- moonlight!

Zephyr's head broke the surface and she could see. But the battle wasn't over. The boat was still there, running lights bobbing. She would have to swim on the surface, fighting the tidal current and towing Rip. There was no way she could do it alone. They would be dashed against the base of the cliff until the sea battered them to death or they drowned.

Then, so abruptly that it frightened her, she felt Rip's lungs expand, squeezing her arm between the weight belt and his ribs. He gasped, coughed, gasped again. The fresh air had revived him.

"Zeph . . . " His voice was so raspy that she could barely hear him over the sound of waves crashing against the cliff.

She spat out the regulator. "Yes, I'm . . . " Water splattered into her mouth, choking off her words. "I'm . . . " She made a little gasping sound. "Here."

"Are . . . are you . . . " He broke off, coughing.

Even with water sloshing in her eyes, she could sense the nearness of the looming cliff. "I'm fine, but we need to just be quiet and kick *hard*!"

With overwhelming relief, she felt the power of his body take over. He was kicking. Her arm, which had been supporting him, became a lifeline between them, holding them together, combining their efforts as if they were one being, one creature swimming for its life.

Slowly, the lights of the boat began to grow nearer. At first, through her salt-scalded eyes, Zephyr thought she had only imagined it, wishing desperately to be nearing its shelter. But, no. The boat, bobbing restless at anchor like a faithful steed straining to aid its master, was distinctly closer. As they kicked away from the cliff, the water gradually grew smoother. Soon they were floating almost comfortably along the winking, moonlit surface.

"Can I talk now?" Rip's voice was weak, but at least reflected his usual strong spirit and sense of humor.

Zephyr coughed and snuffled. "Sure."

"I'm making you an honorary SEAL."

"Me? Why?"

"Because we never leave our buddies behind even if they're dead. You must have thought I was dead, but you didn't give up on me."

"Hey," she said gently, "Don't forget--"

"Forget what?"

"You've got the boat key in your pocket. I wasn't planning to swim all the way back to Lahaina!"

He started to laugh, but water shot up his nose and he coughed instead. "Anyway, you saved my life. If we were Native Americans, I would belong to you."

"Relax. I've never even visited a reservation."

"Was I complaining?"

"I don't know. Were you?"

"Let's discuss it when we get back on board. Just a few more feet. Kick harder."

"You kick harder! *I* got us out of the cave, remember?"

"Always, sweetie. Always. Now grab hold of the swim step."

Flopping and gasping, they dragged and pulled each other onto the bouncing swim step then up onto the deck. For a long time they just lay there in a tangle of arms, legs and half shredded dive gear.

Then Rip sat up and pulled her with him, clasping her against his chest, both of them slippery with water and blood. He kissed her deeply. Their wet lips glided against each other, smooth, hot and sharply salty.

"... I would belong to you ... " Did he mean it?

His fingers twisted in her sodden hair. He stroked the tangled locks away from her face and pressed them back across the top of her head. His comforting hand provided a glorious sensation until pain suddenly shot a hot bolt across her scalp. Her head jerked forward involuntarily.

"What . . . ?" He cupped her chin with his hand and gazed at her. "Did I hurt you?" He felt the back of her head gently. "Oh boy, there's a big knot there! Do you feel okay?"

"I'm fine. It's nothing, really. But let me look at you!" Blinking moisture out of her eyes, she lifted her hand to stroke his cheek. It was sticky with blood. She pulled back to see him better. Even in moonlight, she realized that one of his cheekbones was buried under swelling flesh, the skin rapidly purpling above it. His eye was partly hidden by its swollen lid.

But he was the one who was looking concerned. He took her hand in both of his and it was then that she noticed the blood was coming from her own torn flesh.

He lifted her hand and kissed the battered fingers. "You must have lost your gloves, but you still hung on and got us out of there."

"It's just a few scrapes," she said. "But wait until *you* look in a mirror!" Then, for no reason at all, she began to laugh. She felt the tension that had stiffened her muscles start to lift. "We must look like . . . " She paused to catch her breath. " . . . We must look like a tag team after a losing match!"

"Not tonight, sweetheart. We won this round." He unzipped the top of her wetsuit and lifted the camera strap over her head. "This time you got the camera back to the boat. It even looks like it's in good shape, which is more than I can say . . . " He began to laugh, too. ". . . about the bulldozer engines!"

And they were both laughing madly, sitting on the deck clinging to each other. Rip was the first to regain control. "It'll take Cole Enterprises at least a week to get replacement parts from the Mainland. By that time the beach will be on its way to being listed as vital habitat." He tipped her face up to his, "I think the turtles may have their nesting grounds safe at least a little longer."

Zephyr turned her face away as her chin started to quiver. She felt exhaustion melt her bones and muscles as she leaned into him. Tears brimmed in her eyes, spilled over and mingled with blood and salt water.

"Hey," he said softly, "Hey. Let's get out of this wet stuff."

Leaning on each other, they struggled free of the shredded wetsuits, but when he tried to stand, Rip's knees wobbled. He plopped down again.

"I . . . I guess I did hit my head pretty hard." He bent forward, fighting to get to his footing.

"Let me help you inside." Zephyr hooked her hands under his arms. "Here, lean on me."

"I can walk!" he protested weakly as he dragged himself onto his feet.

"Of course you can. Just not right now."

She lifted his arm over her shoulders. Bracing himself against the bulkhead, he let her steady him as they made their way slowly into the cabin. While he collapsed onto the bunk, Zephyr hurried into the marine head and grabbed two towels. After wrapping the smaller one around her hand, she returned to him and tucked the large towel over his chest. He was shivering.

"We've got to get this wet swimsuit off of you," she said seriously. He looked very pale and his eyes were closed.

His good eye opened and he managed a rakish grin. "I'm not going to stop you," he said.

She put the fingers of her uninjured hand into the waist band and wrestled off the trunks. All the while his smile grew. Unprepared for the effect that seeing his naked body would have on her, she lifted her gaze to his face. Their eyes met and she smiled too.

"Come here, Wonder Woman." He held his arms up and pulled her to him. Her cheek pressed lightly against his swollen one.

"I love you," he whispered into her ear. I've been trying to tell you that, but I didn't think you were ready to hear it."

She took two sharp, uncertain breaths, then murmured, "I am now, because . . . because I love you, too."

And then they were clinging and rolling and somehow her bikini joined his swim trunks on the floor. They were wild with the newness of each other's bodies and the exuberance of having been so close to death and surviving. Combining their minds and will and bodies, they had accomplished something together that neither could have done alone. They had trusted and not been forsaken. They had been one.

Neither of them knew when fatigue overtook them. The only sound was the purring of the kitten who had quietly slipped into the bunk and curled up by the side of two bodies linked together.

12

"Zephyr . . . sweetie . . . wake up."

She opened her eyes. Her head was resting on Rip's shoulder. Snuggled between them, the kitten yawned, stretched, and slipped away in search of his food dish.

"I'm sorry, Zeph." Rip lifted himself on one elbow. "I wish I could let you sleep, but we have to get away from here before it gets light. Karl's company owns a helicopter and they'll be looking for anyone anchored off this end of the island."

She nodded groggily, gradually becoming aware that her hand hurt. "Sure. I know."

She dragged herself off the bunk, then gently helped him sit.

"How do you feel?" she asked anxiously. In the gray, predawn light, he looked terrible.

He leaned forward and hugged her briefly. "Better than I will if we don't get out of here fast. But we need to bandage up your injuries first." He gently picked up her hand and examined the battered flesh.

"See," she said, "it's not even bleeding anymore."

He nodded. "Still, needs bandaging."

With a stifled groan, he stood, crossed the room, and opened the sliding panel to his closet. Among the jumble of clothes he found his first aid kit. Returning to the bunk, he opened the metal box from which he took a tube of antibiotic cream and a roll of gauze. "This will work until we can get you some proper medical attention." He softly kissed her shredded fingertips.

"You, too," she said, touching his cheek. "You need to have a doctor look at that."

He glanced at his wrist watch. "If I don't get us out of here fast, we'll both need more than a doctor!"

■ ■ ■

As the *Ipo Nui* glided over a sea which the setting moon had turned to vanilla cream, the rising sun gradually glazed the water strawberry pink. From where he stood on the bridge next to Zephyr, Rip could see all the way to the pale horizon. The ocean, which had seemed so dreadfully savage a few hours earlier, now stirred gently beneath the boat. In the liquid world of the sea, the constant changes of life were more evident than on the more slowly mutating shore.

Rip steadied the wheel with one hand. His other arm pressed Zephyr against his side. He could hardly process all the changes that had taken place in twenty-four hours.

Now there was the bond of shared danger, the revelation of what they could do together -- of how much stronger they were together than either of them could be apart. But was it enough to base a lifetime on? He thought so. He even dared hope so. Marriage was a scary thought after the disaster with Linda, but Zephyr was different. Even if she was another rich girl, she was different. And he was different. These years of living alone had changed him. Maybe he'd grown up a little. At least he knew enough now not to let any woman use money to try to try to control him. He might be losing his boat, but it was worth it to be free of Jackie's bossiness. He'd save up and someday he'd have another boat. And this time it would be all his.

Zephyr reached up with her bandaged hand and lightly touched his cheek, now roughened by a day's growth of beard. Gently, she turned his face to better examine his swollen eye. "You really do need to see a doctor."

He grinned and shook his head. The movement did hurt but he wasn't about to admit it. "Listen, you're talking to an old veteran here. This is small potatoes compared to some of the wounds I've had. I'll be fine."

He pressed her head against his chest, fingers entwined in her coppery tangle of curls. The boat bounded homeward over water that glittered blue in the light of a new day.

But as they neared the dock in Lahaina, Rip felt his buoyant mood crash around him. A figure was standing on the dock. Tiny and indistinct at first, but as the *Ipo Nui* entered the small harbor and drew closer, he could see with growing distaste that it was the person that he least wanted to see at this moment - Jackie. Beyond her, waiting in the parking lot, was a black and white with two burley Polynesian policemen leaning against it.

"Rip, is that --?" Zephyr's voice was shaking ever so slightly.

"Yep. I guess every silver lining has a black cloud behind it."

"Can't we go somewhere else?"

"I suppose we could dock at Maalaea or even go to Molokai, but that would only postpone the inevitable." He turned to her and managed a smile. "Hawaii is a small state and we haven't got enough fuel to make it to Japan."

"What will they do to us?"

Rip had to admire the way she asked. There was no trace of fear in her voice. He squeezed her shoulder in what he hoped was a gesture of reassurance. "Not 'us' sweetie, just me. You haven't done anything but take pictures, and they don't know about that. Keep it that way. Hide the camera in your duffle. When we land I want you to get your computer and download the footage, then email it to KHNL Honolulu."

"What about you?" Now her voice shook with the fear he hadn't heard before.

He smiled grimly. "Just like Monopoly. It's 'go directly to jail. Do not pass go. Do not collect $200.'" He folded her against him. "But don't worry. You and the video you took are my 'get out of jail free' card. Now can you handle the lines for me?"

Zephyr climbed down the ladder to the main deck. Looking past Jackie she saw another figure moving towards them. The figure was wearing a red and yellow Hawaiian shirt.

Kevin.

As the boat thumped against the dock, she tossed the rope into Jackie's waiting hands. Jackie's mouth was set in a tight line and her lower jaw was thrust aggressively forward. She didn't wait for Rip to descend from the bridge. As soon as the engines were quiet, she jumped on board and began to shout at him, unmindful of the knot of elderly tourists who stood a few feet away waiting for the early morning whale watching boat.

"What the hell were you thinking?" Jackie marched across the deck. Her long blond braid bounced as she walked. "Daddy called half an hour ago. He said someone had sabotaged his bulldozers and I knew right away who that 'someone' had to be! How could you *do* that after I trusted you?"

The group of waiting whale watchers froze. Like a herd of startled deer, all the faces turned as one towards the *Ipo Nui*.

Rip appeared at the top of the ladder staring blandly down at the furiously angry Jackie.

"I have no idea what you're talking about." His voice was dead calm.

"You know perfectly well what I'm talking about you . . . you . . . " She turned to Zephyr as if she'd just registered her presence. "And what is *she* doing here?"

Rip jumped down from the bridge skipping half the rungs and came face to face with Kevin who had hopped on board right behind Jackie.

"Yeah," Kevin yelled, waving a clenched fist. "What *is* she doing here? I stopped by on my way to the airport to give her one last chance, and there's her room -- empty except for a half packed suitcase. I was ready to call the cops. Thought she'd been kidnapped!" He sent a half smile toward Jackie. "Good thing I met this lady in front of the Old Hawaii Inn. When I asked her if she knew where I could find Rip MacKinsey, she said, 'in jail as soon as I catch him.' I figured she was a good person to stick with."

Rip walked past Kevin as if he were invisible, then threw the stern line to a fisherman on the dock. The fisherman whipped the rope around a cleat and stepped back a few feet for a better view of what was occurring on the boat. With a sinking heart, Zephyr saw two Polynesian policemen striding rapidly toward them.

Jackie whirled around and glared at Kevin. "So what's your part in all this?" she snapped.

Kevin gave a sarcastic laugh. "I used to be her fiancée," he said with a gesture in Zephyr's direction. "Now I'm just a guy who missed his flight home. And you are--"

"I'm Rip's ex-partner." She turned and waved her arm to encompass everyone on board.. "And I want all of you to get off my boat *right now*!"

But before anyone could move, the policemen reached the foot of the dock. The taller of the two called out, "Rip MacKinsey?"

With a rueful glance at Zephyr, he answered. "Yes."

"I'm sorry, sir, but we're going to have to place you under arrest for malicious mischief. You need to come down here now." Both of the policemen truly did look regretful. The shorter one removed a pair of handcuffs from his belt.

Silently, Rip stepped down to the dock and, with a resigned shrug, put his hands behind his back. The couples in the whale watching group whispered to each other, eyes wide. Some of the women began to edge away.

Just then a loud snarl of reversing engines announced the arrival of the whale watching boat. It pulled up next to the dock to take on the waiting passengers. The crew quit what they were doing to stare at Rip. One of them, a young man with blond dreadlocks, stopped uncoiling the prow line. He leaned over the railing and called out, "Hey, Rip! Need some help?"

Rip shook his head without looking up.

Jackie continued to shout. "That's right, officers! Take him away, but first get these people off my boat!" She waved again towards Zephyr and Kevin.

"No!" Zephyr stepped forward suddenly. She stared up at Jackie who was half a foot taller than she was. Standing on tip toe, hand on hips, she she spoke in a loud, clear voice. "It isn't yours yet! It's *his* boat because I'm buying out your share and giving it to him. This is his home and his life. He's worked hard for it and you have no right to take it away from him!"

Jackie laughed. She shot Rip a mocking smirk over Zeph's head. "So that's it! You don't need me anymore because you've got yourself another little rich girl to keep you in style! Well it's going to take more than money to get you out of this one, buster!"

Rip was uncomfortably aware of the watching eyes. By tomorrow it would be all over the island. Rip MacKinsey had been bailed out by another rich girl. Another woman was leading him around by the nose. Control. It was all about control.

"Zephyr!" he called out sharply, more sharply than he intended. "Please stay out of this!"

Seeing him standing helplessly there on the dock, arms behind his back, his handsome face bruised and bloody, nearly broke her heart. "No, Rip. I can take care of everything. I'll get the best lawyer I can find!" Her voice shook and she bit her lip in a desperate attempt to stifle a sob.

Rip's impassive coolness vanished. "Zephyr, please!" he shouted. "Just go and do what we talked about -*now*! I can take care of myself!"

The shorter policeman shook his head as though trying to block out the chorus of voices and concentrate on his duties. "You have the right to remain silent. You have the right to an attorney. If you cannot afford one--"

"Forget it. I can afford one!" Rip wasn't looking at the policemen. He was looking straight at Zephyr.

"--one will be appointed for you by--"

"My father has the best lawyers on this island!" Jackie shouted. "They'll see that you stay in jail until Hell freezes over!"

"Yeah! That's right!" Kevin yelled and patted Jackie lightly on her shoulder.

Rip ignored everyone but Zephyr. He kept his one good eye fixed on her. His voice was quiet, but intense. "Zephyr . . . listen . . . to . . . me. Don't do *anything* except what we agreed on. I'll deal with the boat. You just stay out of it. This is none of your business. Go . . . *now*!"

Zephyr nodded, not daring to speak lest sobs burst forth. Why was Rip sounding like a stranger after all they had shared? She swallowed. Her mouth tasted like tears.

"So . . . " Kevin smiled ingratiatingly at Jackie. "You're in luck. I just happen to be a certified scuba dive instructor if you need a replacement for that loser."

No one noticed when Zephyr, duffle bag gripped firmly in her hand, slipped quietly away.

■ ■ ■

At least she'd been almost packed, Zephyr thought as she threw the last tee shirt into her suitcase and snapped it shut. The faster she could get away from here, from Rip, the better. She had to go home. She had to hide. Humiliation burned her to the core as it had the evening when a boy, who had finally managed to break through her wall of shyness long enough to get her to go to the to the senior prom with him, left her alone on the dance floor and spent the evening with another girl. It seemed like forever that she stood at the curb in her expensive prom dress waiting for her mother to pick her up. Sometimes you just have to go home.

When she felt able to control the tremble in her voice, she picked up the house phone and punched "nine."

"Front desk."

"Can you please get me a taxi? I need to go to the airport."

"Certainly. What time is your flight?"

"I . . . I don't know yet. I'm just going to go to the airport and wait until I can get a seat."

"Hummm. Well, you've missed the early morning flight, but there is another one at eleven-forty every day. If you hurry, you might be able to make that one."

"Thanks. I'll try."

She hung up the phone, dragged the suitcase off the bed and set it up on its wheels. She should be feeling great. She'd accomplished the task for which she'd come and more besides. There'd be no more turtle riding. A threat she hadn't even known about - the resort - had been delayed. Maybe it would even be blocked altogether. She'd emailed the video from last night to the television station and received a reply thanking her. After that it would be up to the authorities to protect the nesting ground. Out of her hands.

And Rip would lose his boat. That was out of her hands, too.

It's none of your business!

So he'd said he loved her. So what. She'd been stupid to think that gave her the right to rescue him, to influence the course of his life. This wasn't a book. It wasn't a movie. The words, "I love you," don't imply permanent commitment. Not in this life. Not in the real world.

Twenty minutes later the taxi sped by Oluwalu Beach where Rip had kissed her for the first time. She gazed out at the sparkling bright water, water that she knew so much better than she knew, really knew, the people in her life. Water, life taking, life giving -- a choice. And suddenly the thought came to her -- there are choices everyone must make and they must make them for themselves.

What have I been doing? The whole theme of my life has been rescue. Mother, the sea turtles, now Rip.

" . . . I would belong to you . . . "

She sighed and leaned against the back of the seat, pressing her bandaged hand against her forehead. Obviously, that's what he'd thought. He'd thought she was declaring that he was her property. How had she not understood that? But now it was too late. It was too late to let their relationship develop, to let trust grow. All she wanted now was to hide. She needed to hide from the humiliation and the hurt she'd felt and the hurt she'd inflicted on him, by not understanding.

The island airport was open to the trade winds, soft and warm. Hawaiian music wafted out of speakers and filled the flower-scented air with overwhelming sweetness. She paid the driver, trundled her suitcase to the agricultural inspection, and made her way to the counter.

"Why, yes. We do have a seat available." The dark skinned agent smiled at the computer screen, apparently glad to be able to fill a customer's request. "There was a cancellation, lucky for you!"

Zephyr noticed that the flowers stuck in the woman's thick, dark hair were beginning to wilt. The weather was changing. Today would be hot.

" . . . until we meet again. . . " The disembodied voice of a female vocalist floated down from the dark wooden rafters.

"Okay. I have you confirmed on flight 432. They're already boarding at gate seven, so you need to hurry. Have a nice flight."

Zephyr hitched her purse strap higher on her shoulder and began to walk as fast as her tired, sore muscles would carry her.

Then the heavy scent of flowers grew abruptly stronger. She felt damp petals drop over her head and settle around her neck. Without stopping she glanced down and saw that she was wearing a white ginger lei. She tried to shake it off. It was the tourist treatment like when she'd landed. She hadn't wanted flowers then, either.

"No, thank you." Her voice was brisk. She didn't have time to argue if she was going to catch that flight. She could already see the last of the line disappearing through the gate.

"Okay, get yourself a plastic one, then. But remember I warned you we frown on them --"

That voice, deep and warm. Rip's voice! She whirled around.

" --especially for weddings." He grinned at her. "When Karl heard about the video, he dropped the charges. Now he's busy trying to rehabilitate his image." He touched her shoulder lightly. "I'm sorry I was so harsh with you back at the dock. I asked you once to forgive me, can I ask you again?

"Oh, Rip! I'm the one who needs to be forgiven." She reached up and caressed his swollen, purple cheek. "I shouldn't have tried to rescue you in that way. I have no right to interfere with your life. It's just that money means nothing to me. I have some. You needed it. That's all."

"I know," he said. "We have a lot to learn about each other. If you'll stay here with me we can start to do that. I can't let you buy the boat for me, but I would love to have you as my partner. Could you see yourself doing that?

"Oh Rip! Of course I can!"

He smiled down at her, kissed her tenderly and stroked away the tears that had started to slip out of her eyes.

She looked up at him. His face was so badly battered that it occurred to her that he could even have some broken bones. "We do need to get you to a --"

Then she stepped back and gave a little gasp, covering her mouth with her hand. "Oh, no! There I go again - being the rescuer." She smiled wickedly through her tears. "But if you want to go to the emergency room, I'll be happy to go with you."

He caught her in his arms and pressed her against him. The fragile flowers, crushed between them, poured forth their finest, sweetest perfume.

EPILOGUE

SIX MONTHS LATER
A great, white yacht with its name, *The Seaduction*, written
in tall letters on its stern, scratched a white scar across the
water defacing the reflection of an orange and pink sunset.
A swimsuit clad couple sat in matching canvas deck chairs
while the almost uninhabited south shore of Maui flowed
past. The woman appeared to be concentrating on a navi-
gational chart spread out across her lap.

The man, his blond ponytail emerging from under a
broad brimmed hat, lifted a pair of binoculars to his pale,
blue eyes. He twisted the focusing wheel several times as if
to make sure he was seeing clearly.

"Hey, Jackie, get a look at this!" He stretched out
an arm, prodding the woman's muscular thigh with his
binoculars.

"Oh shut up, Kevin. Can't you see I'm busy? I'm trying
to find that Big Island property Daddy's interested in. It's
the whole reason he sent us the money to come back from
San Diego."

"Sure. Okay. But isn't that the *Ipo Nui* over by Turtle
Beach?

"Give me that!" She dropped the chart, snatched the
binoculars and held them up to her eyes. "Damn. Sure is.
I don't know what they're doing. Now that Zephyr's bunch
of kelp huggers turned the place into a wildlife refuge the

only ones even allowed to walk on that beach are the frigging turtles."

"Well, there's a bunch of folks on board, but I can't tell what's going on . Doesn't look like they've got dive tanks. Give me those a minute!" He made a lunge for the binoculars.

Ignoring him, Jackie stood up and moved towards the railing. The chart fell onto the deck where it rolled itself up. "Humpf," she snorted. "I see somebody in a long, white dress. If that boat weren't Rip's, I'd swear there was a wedding going on. But I know Rip and I know the last thing he'd want on his boat is a wedding. He can't even look at a wedding cake without turning green!"

■ ■ ■

But Rip was, in fact, looking at his bride. His eyes were alight with a deep and abiding love. When she emerged from the cabin of their boat, her beauty had taken his breath away. She was wearing a long, white, off the shoulder muu-muu. Her golden red hair fell softly around her shoulders and curled under a wreath of delicate white flowers.

Rip hadn't wanted a tux, but he was magnificently handsome in white pants topped by a white Hawaiian shirt. His best man, Kawika, stood next to him wearing a similar shirt, but in a much larger size. The minister, who looked as dignified as it was possible to look while standing on the rocking deck of a boat, was also dressed in white. Rip's family and an assortment of friends crowded the benches that rimmed the deck.

As the moon rose, spreading a silvery glow across the water, the beach came alive with hatching baby turtles. Led by ancient instinct, they waddled down the beach and swam away into the dark, mysterious freedom of the sea.